THE INTELLIGENCE GIGANTIC

This elaborate and engrossing story holds the attention of the reader in the firmest possible grip. The Intelligence Gigantic *operates to exceed that of the wisest of humanity and by it the strangest results are brought about. The plot will be found crowded with incident and the reader will be kept in suspense till the very end. This super human intelligence easily takes the lead over mankind at large, and the monster—as he may be called—is virtually without morals and simply embodies pitiless intellectual power, making him a dreadful despot.*

TO
MY MOTHER

Published by
Wildside Press, LLC
P.O. Box 301
Holicong, PA 18928-0301 USA
www.wildsidepress.com

Wildside Press Edition: MMIII

THE INTELLIGENCE GIGANTIC

By

JOHN RUSSELL FEARN

WILDSIDE PRESS

CONTENTS

THREE men stood quietly thoughtful in a wonderfully equipped laboratory, each holding in his hand a sheaf of papers upon which were executed abstruse mathematical formulæ, and sections of the human anatomy, correct to an amazing degree. . . .

The tallest of the three, Doctor Albert Soone, Professor of Chemical Research—a tall, broad-shouldered man of perhaps forty-three years—studied his own papers silently, his lofty forehead wrinkled into furrows of thought, his steel-grey eyes abstracted. The black hair seemed a trifle disordered. . . .

Next to him, equally absorbed, was a much older man, possessing a far kindlier face, less severely chiselled—Professor Peter Ross, Master of Anatomical Research.

The third member of the group, David Elton, an exceptionally well-built young man with riotous fair hair, china-blue eyes, and a square, purposeful face, stood watching his seniors attentively, his hands sunk in the pockets of his laboratory smock. . . .

Presently Dr. Soone laid down his papers on the bench and regarded his two companions meditatively.

"Well, Dave," he remarked at last, after a profound cogitation. "You certainly have found something! Congratulations!"

The words were curtly spoken, in a cold voice. Dr. Soone never enthused over anything, no matter how extraordinary; not for nothing had his contemporaries dubbed him as "cold-blooded."

"Indeed, yes." Professor Ross put down his papers and laid a kindly hand on the young man's shoulder. "My boy, you have undoubtedly discovered something that will raise our race to enormous heights of genius—which will enable us to grow out of our rut of comparatively groping intelligence. Your formula for the creation of a synthetic being, endowed with the power to use its brain to full capacity, should mean an intellectual Titan, dwarfing the most brilliant minds earth has ever evolved."

Dave Elton smiled slightly. "Thanks, Professor. Yet, although I managed to conceive the idea, and work out the formula, I couldn't hope to undertake the task alone. My knowledge of anatomy and chemistry is too slight. That, of course, is why I asked you two gentlemen to become partners with me in giving this creature to the cause of the world's progress."

"Quite," the Professor nodded. "You may rest assured of our most earnest co-operation. Eh, Doctor?"

"Most certainly," Soone agreed; then turning to the young man: "Tell me, Mr. Elton, what started this train of thought? What led up to this startling formula of yours?"

"Well," Dave began, his manner becoming retrospective, "during my college days—I have said already I left about two years ago—I had access to a considerable number of medical books, including *Anatomical Research*, De Sevene's *Theory of Brain Action*, and several others, from which I gleaned positive information that almost every human being has five times as much brain material as he ever uses. It occurred to me that this was odd: why so much waste material? We have ascended from a lower level of creature, according to popular theory; therefore that extra brain-material is certainly not a sort of 'left-over' organism from a more highly developed creature. Is it for future use? Of course we do not know."

"But, gentlemen, Nature does not make mistakes constructing millions of beings with the same brain capacity—therefore, what is missing? I had a discussion with my anatomy instructor over this excess of brain-matter, and between us we found that it is very likely our brain-capacity will always be the same—and remain unchanged far into the future, but, and here is the point, with the passing ages we will become so intellectually perfect that our brains will need use for *all* the material—but the time is not yet. You follow?"

The two men nodded in deep interest, their eyes chained to the bright-eyed young genius before them.

"Well, at the risk of being thought a 'preacher' I'll explain the rest," Dave went on. "I went further into this brain study of mine, made investigations on the mysterious cerebral cortex, studied all about the corpus callosum, which connects the two hemispheres, and pored over the action of nerve-impulses. I just metaphorically dissected a being—and studied him as an engineer studies a delicate machine—to try and find out how the most power could be gained from that extra brain-tissue. I found it was impossible to experiment on a living being, no matter how skilful the surgeon, without causing death. You see, what is lacking with our brains is a nerve connection between the portion of the brain we use and the so-called useless portion. We only think and receive impressions in snatches, imperfectly understood, but—and this is the vital point—with a

[2]

nerve connection to make the entire brain of use, we can operate our brain power to the full! It means a power of thought five times greater than we now have. On that basis I built my formula, which you, Dr. Soone, find to be correct?"

"Perfectly," the famous surgeon and neurologist nodded.

"Good! Well, as I have said, I found it impossible to experiment on a living being because of death. Even if the being should live after the operation, it is possible that this sudden excess of work on the part of the brain might cause such a weakening of the body's other organisms as to bring about death from exhaustion. The only thing, therefore, is to create a synthetic man, built with nerves to stand such immense brain-power—connect up all his brain the way I have outlined, and there he is! An intelligence gigantic! This is your province now, Professor Ross. What we have to do is to duplicate the elements of a human being, and, in a sense, duplicate protoplasm —also reproducing the substance in the nucleus of the body cells —chromatin. Of course, Professor, that part of the business lies with you. I do not know how to reproduce the elements of a human being, or how to endow those elements with the power of life. I have given it as far as I can in my formula, and have shown exactly what organism will have to take the strain of excessive brain power . . ."

The Professor nodded, and deeply thoughtful again studied his papers.

"There is nothing impossible in it, my boy," he said at last, looking up, "but it will take me a little while to prepare the details."

"Of course," Dave nodded. "Time is no object. None of us can work independently of each other. And if this synthetic man is a success it will herald the dawn of a new era! The era of super-intelligent beings! Our intellects will be much belittled by the beings we create, but what of that? If it advances progress what else matters?"

"Have you considered, Dave, that this proposed synthetic being will be—soulless?" asked the Professor quietly. "We cannot make a synthetic soul."

"I think that fact can be discounted," Dave answered. "Soul, in my belief, is nought but the name for certain emotions all occasioned by the brain—good emotions, I consider, are just as natural as, say, the respiratory organs. This being of ours will be both soulless and sexless in the real sense of the word—yet I am willing that he shall have no more tendencies towards cruelty than his natural, less intelligent, counterparts."

[3]

"Hmm—maybe," the Professor assented with a shrug, but his grey eyes reflected a shade of doubt. "It, of course, remains to be seen."

"I support Dave's view," said the Doctor methodically. "I also believe that the various sentiments we attribute to an enigmatic 'soul' are really only normal bodily impulses—as yet imperfectly understood."

Ross shook his head. "I just can't see it that way, my friends. Soul is God-given, not to be tampered with by the hands of man. Nature has set the seal of invisibility upon soul—no man can understand or interfere with it. It is shielded from us by an unbreakable barrier of God-like purity. It is an—an infinite 'something' we all possess in a greater or lesser degree. But of course"—he smiled slightly—"my views need not enter into this matter."

"They certainly will not, Professor," remarked Soone coldly. "We have too much before us to allow personal opinions to influence the matter in the slightest!"

Ross looked surprised for a moment, then he shrugged indifferently.

"Suppose we leave it at that, then?" Dave said, looking at his companions each in turn. "It will take you both a little while to work your respective systems out—and, of course, this laboratory of mine is at your disposal to serve for whatever you wish, and whenever you wish. I will acquaint Jesmond with that fact, and he will make arrangements for you both to have admittance whenever you desire it. . . . When shall we meet again to officially discuss the final details?"

"I shall be ready in—a week," replied Ross, musing. "I have a great deal to work out, but I think a week will amply cover it. How about you, Doctor?"

"Quite suitable for me. We'll call it seven p.m. this day week, shall we?"

"Right!" Dave responded. "And let us hope for success, gentlemen."

"There is no reason to anticipate failure, Dave," Ross said confidently. "Between us we will create a master-mind or—as you have said—an intelligence gigantic!"

After the two scientists had departed, Dave Elton went slowly and thoughtfully towards his library, his mind turning over all that had been done and said during the past few hours. He paused with his hand on the library door as Jesmond, his one man servant, came towards him in characteristic swift silence.

"Miss Conisbery is in the library, sir," he announced

smoothly. "She came about half an hour ago, and when I informed her that you were engaged in the laboratory she said she would not disturb you, and decided to wait."

"Very well, Jesmond, thank you. Oh, by the way, it is highly probable that Dr. Soone and Professor Ross may frequently come up to the laboratory. Even if I am absent, please allow them perfect liberty to use everything here."

"Certainly, sir. Will there be anything further?"

"No, not at present. Thanks."

Dave entered the library, extending his hands in greeting as a girl of about his own age rose from the arm-chair by the fire and came quickly towards him with a tripping step.

"Dave Elton, you have kept me waiting half an hour!" she exclaimed in mock reproof, as he cupped her two hands in his.

"What have you got to say for yourself after forgetting that I was waiting for you?"

The young man laughed, then he quietly studied the girl for a moment—the deep violet eyes and extraordinary golden hair, the straight, aristocratic nose and sensitive mouth, with the determined little chin, entirely devoid of dimples, giving a suggestion of strong will and certainty of purpose.

"Nan, do you mean to say that after three years you still pull me to attention when I have important business on hand?" he asked sternly. "Shame on you, child!"

"Well, am I not important?" she pouted at him. "If you behave like this when we've only been engaged three months, what are you going to be like when we're married?"

Then, unable to restrain themselves, they both burst into laughter.

Together they went over to the settee and sat down.

"Well," Dave asked, putting his arm about her shoulders, "and what brings you here, Nan?"

"Purely the fact that I was passing on my way up to town, so I thought I'd call in and discover how your mysterious secret is progressing," she replied a trifle vaguely; then smiled disarmingly. "Tell me, Dave, what this secret is—please!" and the entreaty she succeeded in putting into her unfathomably blue eyes destroyed all the reserve Dave ever possessed.

"I'm sorry, Nan, if I've not revealed anything so far," he said contritely, "but to tell the truth, I had to be quite sure of the co-operation of two famous scientists before I could say anything."

"And have you got that co-operation now?"

[5]

"Yes—that's what I was doing this afternoon. You've heard of Dr. Albert Soone and Professor Ross?"

"Yes—but—— What on earth have you discovered, Dave, to require the services of such men? I know you're wealthy, but—don't their fees run high?"

Dave laughed heartily. "Bless your heart, Nan, they're only too glad to help me—*gratis*. You see, we three are now going to work together in turning a theory of mine into a possibility. Namely, old girl, we're going to create a gigantic intellect—a human being, with a brain of tremendous power."

"A—a what?" the girl repeated, obviously startled, looking at him with wide eyes.

"A synthetic being, Nan—the first living creature to be born independent of another human being—a creature of flesh and blood like you or me, but with an intelligence exceeding yours or mine five times over. You see, it is like this . . ." and he went off into one of those moods of technical fecundity for which he was remarkable.

When he had concluded the girl sat in silence for a time, and Dave fancied he saw her face harden slightly. Surely, he reflected, it must have been a trick of the dancing firelight. Her next words astounded and completely disillusioned him. They fell upon him like sudden ice and robbed him of every conception.

"Dave, I never thought you capable of such a thing!" she said, and her tones were low and cutting. "Whilst I admit your brilliance, your undeniable genius, in conceiving such a being with a super-intelligence, you have forever destroyed my faith in you as a good-living, right-thinking, honest young man! What you have planned, and what those two scientists have agreed to, is blasphemy! I do not hesitate at saying it!"

"But, Nan, if only you——"

"Let me finish!" the girl requested stonily. "Science is undoubtedly the mainstay of human progress, but when it comes to creating living beings, and endowing them with an intellect beyond that planned by Nature, it is grotesque. You have no right to do it!"

"I don't see why not!" Dave returned obstinately. "It's for the advancement of the human race."

"You are so blind as that!" Nan exclaimed in amazement; then she shook her head slowly. "Then I may just as well save my breath, Dave. If you must have your science, Nature at least ought to escape your dabbling hands. You're going to create a monster, Dave—in all seriousness you are!"

[6]

Dave did not answer.

"Intellectually colossal, I know," she said quietly; "but at the cost of a soul it's not worth it."

"Like Frankenstein's monster, eh?" Dave asked dryly. "You've got the old idea into your head that a laboratory-made creature must be without a soul. I don't believe that at all . . . Nan, why can't you leave it all to me? What has my work got to do with all we have in common?"

"The work you do must, of necessity, reflect the character you possess, since you do that work from choice," the girl answered, looking away. "As a man, you probably think you are justified in what you are doing—but to me, a woman, your plans seem vile. You propose breaking the very laws which govern life. . . ." Quite abruptly she rose to her feet and straightened her costume. "No, Dave," she said firmly, "this finishes everything between us. I cannot have anything in common with a man who seeks to create an intellectual monster. My whole woman's being cries out against it!"

Dave was on his feet now. He seized the girl's slim shoulders in broad, powerful hands. "Do you mean that you leave me— leave me flat, as they call it—if I go on with this work?"

"I do, Dave." The purposeful face was set and determined. "Do not imagine it is easy, Dave. As a man I love you with all my heart and soul—but as a scientist, I hate you! It's either I or science. Choose."

A silence fell between them. Dave's face reflected in turn all the emotions of a man passing through an intense mental struggle. Then with a sudden curious gentleness he dropped his hands from the girl's shoulders and looked away.

"I cannot back out now, Nan," he said hopelessly. "The whole scheme is launched—like a machine in which the cogs are moving and cannot be stopped. And, anyway"—his tone took on fierceness and the blue eyes flamed—"I consider I've been mistaken in you, Nan! It's your sort that forever hinders progress and drops stumbling-blocks and barriers in the path of progress. Instead of standing by me and helping me, all you can do is to air your own petty views, and claim priority because you happen to be a woman. Well, you can get on with it! My Intelligence will be created, and when you see the benefits that follow you'll come and ask my forgiveness. . . ."

"Quite well recited—and you flatter yourself, too," the girl returned, with polished acidity. "That Intelligence of yours will bring only destruction. Good-bye."

She swung round on her heel and made for the door.

"But, Nan——" Dave exclaimed hoarsely, dazed by her sudden departure and the infinite coldness with which she was taking it. "Nan! I didn't mean all of that——" He stopped dead as the door slammed behind the girl's unheeding ears. . . .

The same evening, by the last post, a locally stamped letter arrived for Dave. Moodily he tore the flap, and from the envelope extracted a narrow ciclet of gold, with three bulging diamonds clawed thereon. A little slip of notepaper, emanating the faintest hint of an elusive perfume, bore upon its delicate surface the following words . . .

"Remember, I still love David Elton the man—but I hate, loathe, and detest David Elton the scientist. You know what to do—until then I refuse to even hear from you!

"Nancy Conisbery."

Quietly Dave put the ring in his wallet, smiled faintly and dejectedly at the little note, so small yet so powerful—then, with a sudden unreasoning savagery he kicked the foot-stool at his feet and flung the waste-paper-basket across the library.

"Dave!" he breathed hotly. "What a damn fool you are!"

CHAPTER II   *The Making of the Intelligence*

A FEW days of comparative idleness, a moody reflection on his own shortcomings and brutal outspokenness, then Dave Elton was back again at his work, having, as he believed, successfully steeped himself so deep in his scientific pursuits that the thought of Nancy Conisbery did not create the slightest fluctuation in his mentality. He viewed her as a girl with oddly perverted ideas, as an annoying distraction in his efforts to progress, as one who claimed first right because she was a woman. He grunted as the unbidden vision of her obtruded through the accumulating mass of mental, scientific facts—he almost cursed aloud as unconsciously he went over that last interview with her in his mind's eye. Each time, it seemed, he saw himself more objectionable, more ruthless, more of a machine than a man. . . . There were even times when he debated the fact that she might have seen further into the future than he did when she foresaw the Intelligence as a devouring monster and a destroyer of all cherished attainments and rosy ideals. . . .

"Bosh!" said Dave harshly, and turned back to his interrupted work, only to trail off in absent-minded contemplation of the small circlet of gold he had taken from his waistcoat pocket. . . .

Right on time, one week later, Dr. Soone and Professor Ross arrived—the Doctor as saturnine and curt as ever, whilst Ross was as mildly enthusiastic as his mature years permitted.

In the laboratory he made his conclusions clear.

"Rather contrary to your beliefs, Dave, we have not reproduced protoplasm, but rather the elements of a human being," he said sonorously, as though delivering a lecture. "By the blending of the elements and atoms that make a human being we have, as it were, the framework of our experiment. Next, we have to reproduce the same chemical element, the same reaction, that started life on this planet of ours. As our synthetic man takes on shape we can strengthen those nerves which will take the strain of tremendous brain-power, and so, finally, by linking up all the brain-cells, complete our creature. My calculations—here they are—show that metabolism will be extremely rapid. Within a month or six weeks our man will have evolved from the first elements to adult life—only differing in three ways from ourselves—his enormous range of thought, his complete lack of sex, and his absolute absence of—soul!

"Actually to set up all the material necessary should not take more than five hours. Afterwards, it will be just a case of tremendous, unceasing growth, as he swells from babyhood to maturity. We could make him grown up right away, but I don't altogether hold with that idea. Going from the lesser to the greater he will have the time to develop his faculties and enormous mental resources. Food he will have to get in plenty, in order to replace the enormous waste occasioned by such tumultuous growth. After all, there is no reason to suppose but what he will eat like you or me. That, I think, covers everything."

"What do you propose to create him in?" asked the Doctor.

"A glass case, shielded from the air of the laboratory, and heated in the interior to 98° Fahrenheit," the Professor replied. "As he grows, the temperature will be lowered until it equals that of our own air."

"What sort of glass?" Dave inquired. "Why glass at all?"

"Merely ordinary quarter-inch glass, but the case must be made to design. The reason for using glass is so that we may see what is transpiring inside. Another reason is, so that the

[9]

special combination of rays we shall use, to excite the chemical reaction, will pass through."

"Suppose our creature does not evolve into a man, but something else—say, a dog—or even an unfathomable monstrosity?" the Doctor enquired. "What then?"

"It is very unlikely," returned Ross. "In every detail we are supplying the elements which go to make a human being—whereas the elements of a bird, animal, or fish, are quite different. Nearly all human beings have two legs, two arms, and a trunk—the body—such is the outcome of the conditions of our planet. Even if by some mischance our creature should show signs of becoming something hideous, we have simply to create synthetic parts to replace the wrong ones."

"Only one thing puzzles me," Dave remarked. "At this rate, our creature will be no more intelligent than we are."

"Evidently I have not made myself clear. The brain of this creature will be placed in position as soon as the elements take on form. That will be the Doctor's task. That intellect will have to be connected up in much the same way as a radio engineer connects a wireless apparatus."

"During that process, then, I take it that the rays causing chemical reaction will be cut off, and the creature will cease temporarily to grow?"

"Exactly. When the Doctor has completed his task growth will resume its course."

"But, until it is taught it will not understand anything," Dave objected. "We hadn't considered that."

"It will not require teaching, any more than a real infant needs to be taught to cry. It will read and learn by studying *our* minds. And it will easily have the power to do it. After that, it's just a case of accumulating more and more knowledge."

"I see. And what will be the nature of the rays to cause the chemical reaction?" Doctor Soone asked, in his level voice. "Duplication of solar rays? They, obviously, are the root of our life."

"The point is, *are* they?" said Professor Ross broodingly. "In the dim ages of the Beginning, how do we know that it *was* solar power that started life? Some condition of earth itself might have done it. . . . I have not yet solved that problem—the most vital problem of all. We cannot excite life in lifeless atoms and molecules, until we know what reaction does it. I shall go over my equations again and try and evolve the right formula. We have everything . . . but that."

*   *   *   *   *

It was two days later when the three met again.

"I believe I have it!" declared the Professor triumphantly. "You were right, Doctor Soone. Solar rays are responsible for the evolution of protoplasm—but only certain of those rays."

"I could hardly conceive of anything else being the reactive agent," returned the Doctor coldly.

"The rays, I believe, which cause the reaction, are those which contain a high percentage of electricity, which disrupt the atoms of matter and release the power known as life. Two other rays are also indispensable—one is in the ultra-violet. As this loses its power when passing through glass we must arrange for a direct beam. The other one is of a frequency below ultra-violet, whilst the electrical ray itself is above ultra-violet. The combination of all three, my calculations tell me, should create *life! Life!* We will start about equipping a ray machine right away. When it is finished we'll test the rays on some of our material. If it releases the chemical reactivity, we're well on the road to success. Come, let us make plans—for the ray machine and the special glass case. . . ."

A fortnight of feverish activity followed on the part of these three scientific men, who sought to improve a world deficient in intellectual attainments. Having, as it were, a definite line of action upon which to work, they laboured with that curious tirelessness common to the scientific profession, until at the end of fourteen days, weary at last with the strain, they had concluded the manufacture of the Ray Machine, of the special glass case, eight feet long by three wide (with an orifice in the side for the insertion of the Ray Machine's ultra-violet quartz lens), and the manufacture of artificial protoplasm. This latter contained mainly haphazard elements and gases. It might evolve into anything. The Professor had not concerned himself with duplicating the elements of anything in particular for the first experiment.

Doctor Soone looked at the small mound in the base of the glass case, and then at the Ray Machine, the lenses on its snout-like front pointed towards it.

"Proceed, Professor," he said in level tones. "Ready, Dave?"

"Absolutely!" Dave returned tensely.

The Professor's hand trembled slightly as he threw in the switch of the machine. A pale violet ray, fringed along its edges with the remotest suggestion of yellow, sprang from the central lens and focused upon the little heap in the centre of the case. . . . In a far corner of the laboratory the generators of the Ray Machine hummed rhythmically. . . . In his usual methodic, precise fashion the Doctor inspected the thermometer and air pressure gauge on the side of the case, and pronounced them satisfactory. Then hands in pockets, he turned his steel-grey eyes to a silent contemplation of the substance within the case.

For fully twenty minutes nothing happened. The Professor's face became a study in suspense and concentration of effort; Dave's frowning and intent; whilst on the hard visage of Soone there lurked the incipiency of a sardonic smile. . . .

Then all three suddenly sprang to attention and stared fixedly. The mound had moved . . . jumped! It was twitching, like some phantasm of a nightmare. The Professor breathed hard as he played the rays unceasingly into the case.

Time passed on, and with astounding rapidity the substance grew and enlarged, until finally it was a perfect oval. It pulsated steadily.

With an inarticulate exclamation Professor Ross shut off the machine.

"My God!" he muttered. "It lives!" For a moment he felt like one who has committed some diabolical outrage.

The oval having ceased to grow, lay like a cocoon on the floor of the case. The distinct beating of some hidden heart was evidenced by the steady and deliberate pulsation on the tight, hairless skin of the Thing.

"This—this seems incredible!" Dave almost whispered. Then he suddenly looked up, startled. "It's stopped pulsating! Yes! Look!"

"Exactly," nodded the Doctor calmly. "For the simple reason that it has been starved. It should have been nourished as we proceeded, Professor. Injections should have been given. We must guard against this when we create the Intelligence."

"Yes. Indeed we must," rejoined Professor Ross.

The Professor spoke slowly and absently. He seemed a trifle dazed by the amazing thing his hands had perpetrated. Yet there could be no doubt about it. The combined immutable laws of chemistry, physics, and mathematics could not lie. For a long time he stood gazing down at the now inanimate, shapeless thing.

"Well?" asked the Doctor at last, somewhat curtly. "What's troubling you now, Professor?"

"Just the fact that the Intelligence will have no soul," the elderly scientist replied quietly, dubiously shaking his head. "Somehow I have a feeling that we are meddling in affairs that will prove too much of a handful for us."

"My—er—fiancée broke our engagement for the same reason," Dave remarked sombrely.

"She did!" The Professor shrugged and looked broodingly into the glass case again. "A woman's intuition often reaches farther than all the forecasts of science, Dave."

"Rubbish!" snapped the Doctor impatiently. "Have you never heard of conservatism?—that sense of unconscious obtinacy—which refuses to credit anything a little removed from the conventional? That is all the views of your fiancée amount to, Dave. To make a success of this experiment we cannot afford to allow any adverse opinions to deter our purpose."

"I'll thank you, Doctor, to leave my fiancée out of the argument," Dave returned in a quietly firm voice.

Soone shrugged his shoulders indifferently. "Pray accept my apologies, Dave, for anything I may have said, which offends your—er—naturally sentimental emotions towards your fiancée. I do not imply by that, however, that I do not mean what I have said. I did mean it. We have got to look at this matter squarely. We cannot back out now."

"I, for one, have no intention of backing out," said the Professor, with dignity.

"Just as well," Soone commented in an off-hand fashion. "If you do back out I shall be compelled to make the Intelligence on my own account. Remember I know the full formula."

"I am aware of that," the Professor returned dryly. "As I have no intention of backing out, however, we had better make our plans for the creation of the Intelligence itself."

"It would perhaps be as well," Soone acceded.

At precisely three o'clock the following afternoon, January 19th, 2038, the creation of the Intelligence commenced. . . .

The differences of opinion that had characterized the earlier experiments seemed swallowed up now in the dawn of the miracle. . . .

In the base of the glass reposed the substance which, according to formula, should evolve into a human being. When everything was finally in order the three relapsed into dead silence. Quietly the Professor switched on the Ray Machine, and, as before, that pale violet ray fringed with yellow impinged upon and held the substance in the base of the case.

Dave shifted somewhat uneasily and watched intently. The Doctor carefully looked over the organic compounds and liquids that were to be used in the nourishing of the creature. Only the throbbing generators disturbed the aching silence.

[13]

Minutes passed—minutes of such infinite and appalling suspense as the three had never experienced in their lives before. . . . Then, suddenly, the incredible happenings of yesterday! The substance moved, gyrated in an astounding fashion, came to rest, and commenced to swell, slowly but perceptibly. . . .

It took on outlines.

"Feed it! An injection, Soone!" panted the Professor, and shut off the machine for a moment.

The Doctor instantly obeyed, performing the operation by using a syringe through india-rubber vacuum traps in the case, which, whilst permitting room for his arms, stopped all exit of the case's inner air, or any entrance of the outer air. . . .

The work went on. Slowly the growth of the creature continued. By gradual degrees the substance changed from complete shapelessness into understandable formation.

It became manifest, as time passed, that work would have to go on ceaselessly for fourteen days at the least, therefore a hasty scheme of shifts was decided upon. Dave gave the necessary instructions to the unmoved Jesmond and accommodation was arranged. . . .

The next day the creature had formed. Perpetual injections alone kept this mite of synthetic matter alive. . . . With growing wonder at the fantastic thing they had done, the three scientists silently viewed the creature from time to time. . . .

On the fourth day the Doctor performed the delicate operation of providing the creature with the synthetic brain. With the skill of a master-hand he connected up the vital nerves and cells, and provided the communication to the large "waste" tissue from the usual brain section. . . . After that, the creature just grew . . . and *grew!*

A week later the temperature of the case was lowered to that of the laboratory. The ray still played upon the creature—but now it was, to all intents and purposes, a normal child of perhaps twelve years old, with perfect physique and extraordinary development of forehead. The eyes of the creature were a deep and lustrous black and had already taken on a quality of extreme penetration. To meet the direct gaze of the creature caused strange mental perturbations in the minds of the three scientists. It seemed as though intellectual power had been sapped from them—and, in truth, it had. From their minds the astounding creature was learning all the knowledge that it would take many long years to even teach an ordinary child. . . .

"He's going to be a super-genius," muttered the Professor, on the ninth day. "I almost feel we've been justified, Soone."

"I know it," the taciturn surgeon answered. "Nothing will ever convince me otherwise."

"And I, too, think Nan must have been mistaken," murmured Dave reflectively. "I do not credit, gentlemen, that I got the idea for this creature, unless it was intended I should develop it. We are going to give to the world a wonderful intelligence, who will set our differences in order."

"We trust so," assented the Professor, but that same doubting tendency crept unbidden into his tone. ...

*   *   *   *   *

After another six days had passed the finished product of three brilliant minds stepped forth from the glass case, and was duly supplied with suitable attire. ...

The Intelligence stood about five feet eight inches tall, with broad, though not unusually massive shoulders. In every detail he was perfectly formed. The face was singularly square and expressionless, ivory white—the lips were thin and set in an even, straight line. ... Black hair, smooth as silk, lay flattened back from a forehead of amazing width and height.

From every aspect it was a face that portrayed nothing more or less than cold, ruthless calculation and absolute barrenness of all sentiment. It had upon it the unpleasant stamp of incarnate materiality. In some inexplicable way it reflected the government of a man's hand; there was a complete absence of even that vestige of compassionate insight discernible on even the cruellest human face. ...

The Professor regarded this iron visage almost sadly. A light of disappointment crept into his thoughtful eyes. It was as though he viewed something entirely different from what he had expected, something unspeakably repulsive, something bearing the irremovable mark of the beast.

The Doctor was placidly complacent; Dave somewhat thoughtful and detached, as though unable to reach an opinion. ... Somehow the Intelligence did not please him. The quality of ruthlessness and materiality embodied in the creature was oddly revolting. The delicate, inimitable touch of Nature herself was missing. All the crudities of a man's hand and the non-intelligent products of a laboratory were reflected in this, the first synthetic man.

Each of the scientists still found it difficult to look for more than a few moments at a time into the creature's profound black eyes. In their abysmal depths smouldered a peculiar green fire, akin to that in an animal's when seen in the gloom.

[15]

"Gentlemen," said the Intelligence at last, in a slow, unemotional, completely mechanical voice, "you have created me from artificial products, and by artificial means. You have endowed me with an intelligence five times greater than your own. From your minds I have already discovered the entire state of this planet, and the so-called intelligence of the beings which populate it. In addition, I have read and can speak every language on this earth. Your highest mathematical computations are extraordinarily childish and really quite amuse me. All that the intelligence on this planet has ever conceived I mastered whilst in the creating case, and have gone much further! Really, you are all very low in the scale of intellect."

"We know that," returned the Doctor steadily; "but kindly do not forget that we had the intelligence to create *you!*"

"I have not forgotten that," returned the Intelligence in the same steely tones. "It was a childish task. Obviously you had only to duplicate your own body elements, evolve same by ultra-violet and Z-rays, and then constantly inject organic compounds. Childishly simple."

"To you, maybe," Soone replied. "To us—difficult."

"I wonder if I may test your intelligence?" Dave asked, rising from his thoughtful contemplation of the creature.

"You may ask what you please," the cold voice answered. "I have already read your questions from your mind—but proceed."

"Well, simple ones first. I have a watch in my pocket which you have never seen. What is its number?"

"4613912," answered the creature instantly. "Slightly marked on the glass, solid gold, bequeathed to you by your father, Daniel Elton."

"Correct. Now a few teasers. What is the fourth dimension?"

"The fourth dimension is the velocity of space, which subdivides into the fifth and sixth dimensions. In all there are eighteen dimensions to the universe. I will work them out for you——"

"No, thanks," Dave interjected hurriedly. "What is the 'velocity of space,' anyhow? I'm a scientist, but I've never heard of that."

"You would not understand it. *This* is the fourth dimension——" and so saying the intellectual Titan stepped aside, and vanished!

"He's gone!" ejaculated Dave hoarsely. "Quick, we must——"

"Wait!" came the familiar metallic voice from the air itself. "I am in the fourth dimension, and, should I choose, I could move backwards and forwards in Time, which is in relation to it at right angles. Time is the fifth dimension, and the composition of Time is the sixth dimension. As all are purely mathematical concepts I doubt if you can understand it . . ." Followed a vague thudding noise and the Intelligence was before them again.

"You see, gentlemen, the knowledge of how to enter and leave the fourth dimension is extraordinarily simple. Let me work it out for you in equations."

"It would be quite useless," returned the Doctor quietly. "What is child's play to you in mathematics would baffle us completely."

The Intelligence shrugged. "Very well, gentlemen. Regrettable, but evidently unalterable. . . . I must leave you all shortly and go out into this strange, barbaric world which you are pleased to imagine is in a condition of comparative perfection. It must all be altered—improved, and I will be the being to improve it!"

"But you can't go straight out into the world and start upsetting laws and rules that have been maintained for generations," Dave exclaimed, startled, seizing the Intelligence's arm.

"And why not?" the cold voice asked. "You created me to improve the world."

"Yes, but—but in a certain way, in a manner which will not upset the community at large," returned the Professor.

The brooding eyes turned to him. "I care nothing for laws and rules! Laws of fools made for fools! They are going to be swept aside! Whatever blocks my path shall be mowed down, without mercy or question. I am going to become the ruler of this odd planet first, choose a few of your so-called highest minds, and train them to understand the New Era. I do not desire your aid—indeed I have no use for it. You are too intellectually feeble."

"Wait!" urged the Professor, horror in his voice. "If you carry out this plan of yours you are going to upset the whole world! You *must* listen to us! We are your masters!"

The Intelligence did not laugh; he did not seem to possess any known emotion. Only the same inflexible voice replied: "I admit no masters! My only master is the one who has a greater mind than I have! Find that—and I am under control!"

The three scientists looked at each other in bafflement. All their treasured plans of using the Intelligence to improve such matters as they deemed advisable seemed to be going astray. With a sudden cold shock of alarm they realized that they had failed to include one factor—that the Intelligence would possess an individuality of his own. . . .

"You can't! You mustn't!" declared the Professor suddenly, with a vehemence that seemed curiously pitiful. "If you dare to move out of this laboratory we will have to use force—by magentized rods, whose power you cannot escape!"

"There is no power you can devise that can retain me," the stony voice rejoined. "I am going, and now—but we have not seen each other for the last time."

"Stop!" thundered the Professor, and stood erect and commanding.

The Intelligence, who had half turned aside, moved slowly back again to face the elderly scientist. The deadly eyes of the being slowly opened to their full capacity and the green fire in their depths smouldered more brightly for a brief instant. . . . Before the startled eyes of Soone and Dave the old scientist gently sagged forward and collapsed upon the concrete floor without a sound. . . .

"Good God!" Dave muttered aghast; then he rushed forward and dropped to his knees by the Professor's side. As he looked up at the Doctor there was an astounded look in his eyes.

"Dead!" he breathed huskily. "Soone, he's stone-dead!"

"He stood in my way; I destroyed him with the force of my mind," said the unmoved Intelligence, looking down at the still figure of the scientist. . . .

At these words there slowly crept into the face of Dr. Soone an expression of awe, suddenly supplanted by cunning.

"A being who can kill by mind-force represents the power of which I have often dreamed," he murmured. "A force that can conquer a world." He straightened up suddenly and purposefully. "Listen to me! I am willing to assist you, Intelligence, in whatever attempts you intend to make to conquer the world . . . this absurd world, with its childish whims and idiotic conventions. You have my word on unswerving allegiance."

"I see in your mind that you are a trainable type," the Intelligence responded. "You have little sentiment; you are coldly calculating, and are not given to that peculiar emotion, fear. Come!"

"Wait a minute!" snapped Dave, jumping up and seizing the Doctor's arm fiercely. "What do you mean by this, Soone?

Look what a mess I'm going to be in! I might be accused of—murder!"

"Maybe," the Doctor nodded callously. "At a time like this, however, it's every man for himself. I choose the Intelligence. You see," he added, with a sardonic chuckle, "he's safer!"

"Why, you infernal——" Dave commenced savagely, then he stopped dead in his sudden forward rush as the Doctor and the Intelligence stepped to one side and disappeared.

"Good day, Dave," came the Doctor's slowly fading voice.

"We leave you, *via* the fourth dimension. But only for a while. . . ."

Dave cursed aloud.

It seemed as though a malignant fate was resolutely determined to hound him down for the amazing thing his mind had conceived. . . .

CHAPTER III   *Nan Returns*

THE weeks that followed the disappearance of Dr. Soone and the Intelligence were grim ones for Dave Elton. Almost before he realized it he was in the midst of a murder case, on trial for his life, for the murder of Professor Ross. . . . He found himself in a position of singular danger, chiefly by reason of his resolve to reveal nothing of the making of the Intelligence. He realized with intense clearness that the law would place no belief in such a fantastic story; if anything, it would only tend to make the case against him all the blacker. Indeed the unpleasant fact that he might be certified insane was not impossible. . . .

The technicalities of the law proceeded with a monotonous, ruthless deadness. Explanation and examination took their respective turns. By degrees Dave's career was undermined, his personality was verbally thrashed out and beaten—all his morals, his attributes, his brilliant accomplishments, were stripped from him like a cloak. . . . Then, out of the maze of intricate details, steeped as they were in accusation and circumstantial evidence, there emerged a pathologist—a Dr. Casby, who, with an extraordinary brilliance and vivid eloquence, proclaimed that his examination of the dead Professor had revealed a brain trouble of unusual characteristics.

It was this which had killed the old scientist.

From the dock, Dave stared at this eloquent little man as

though dazed. The sentences flowed from the lips of this curiously indistinguished pathologist, as though uttered by vocal organs other than his own. The grey eyes stared away into vacancy, the arms moved as though by machinery. To the scientific eyes of Dave it became gradually obvious that the pathologist was completely hypnotized by some stupendous mental force. He spoke by the commands of another will—he moved by the orders of that same obscure mental force. . . .

Dave wrestled with the mystery alone; he lost all sense of time as days went by, until at last, through the low murmurs of the court's intercourse came a clear "Not guilty!"—vivid and sharp, cutting like a knife on that murmurous undercurrent.

Dave dimly saw the little pathologist, whose astounding powers had saved his life and name, disappear among the crowd in the court . . . and all his efforts to reach him, to communicate with him and learn the true circumstances, were in vain.

    *   *   *   *   *

Several days after the trial Dave had somewhat recovered from his ordeal, and endeavoured to hold his mind down to the task confronting him. To fight it alone, however, seemed a task of such colossal proportions that at first he shied at it. He spent a day roaming the countryside and returned in the early evening. The harsh cold of the winter had passed now and the early March evenings were unusually mild. A sickle moon gleamed blue-white over the orange afterglow in the west.

Quietly Dave sank down on the grass of the meadow at the rear of his home gazing despondently into the stillness.

"Why the devil did I ever create such a thing?" he muttered, half aloud. "I think—in fact I'm sure—that Nan must have been right! I'm so utterly alone—the one man in the world who knows what is coming, and I have nobody to confide in. How on earth I'm ever going to get over such a problem alone I can't conceive. . . ."

He drew out his pipe and slowly filled the bowl. In the same meditative fashion he lit up and puffed the blue smoke into the windless air. One by one, as he sat on thinking, the stars gleamed forth above him.

"No," he muttered at last. "Alone, I cannot do it!"

He slowly rose to his feet, still contemplative. Turning, he made to walk toward his home, when a dim figure, small yet compact, barred his path.

"Why—Nan!" he gasped, taking his pipe from between his teeth. "What in the world are you doing here? Jove, but I'm glad to see you! I—I've never wanted so much to talk to somebody who understands in all my life!"

The pale light of the late evening sky faintly illumined the girl's face. The soft wind, bearing a promise of early spring, touched and moved a tiny golden curl that peeped from beneath her hat. It struck Dave that her face seemed pale.

"Dave," she said, in her low sweet voice, "I *had* to come! I've tried to keep away—to keep to what I said in my letter, but somehow—— Oh, I couldn't! I know what you've been going through at the murder trial. I just had to see you! I've been standing here some little time; I overheard your early remarks. But, Dave, you will not have to struggle alone. I want to struggle with you, if you'll let me," she added almost shyly.

"Let you!" Dave exploded, jamming his pipe in his pocket. "Good Lord, Nan, you've dropped right from Heaven! Why, with you beside me I could conquer the earth! Come inside, though, and I'll tell you all about it over a supper. It's getting dark out here."

He led the way into the house, talking vaguely the while, hinting at technicalities the girl could not even hope to understand.

"Now listen, Dave," she said quietly, when they were seated at a cosy supper, "you know I've not the vaguest idea what those scientific terms of yours refer to. Suppose we get down to something practical." Decisively she sipped her coffee.

Dave smiled a trifle ruefully. "You're right, Nan. I'll try and talk in plain language. You see, I made the Intelligence after all, despite your warning. But now—— Well, I'm thinking you were right!" He clasped his hands and stared moodily at the girl across the table.

Nan sighed impatiently. "Come now, Dave, don't get morbid! Drink your coffee before it cools. Remember, I'm here to help you, but I can't do it whilst you dash off unfinished sentences here and there and leave me to conjecture the remainder. You say that you created the Intelligence. Well, how did that cause you to be accused of—murder? It's a harsh word, I know, but we understand each other. Come, tell me."

"Well, the Intelligence, it seemed, was determined to rule the earth, but old Professor Ross stood in his way and ordered him to obey the commands we gave him. In response, the Intelligence—the damnable Colossus of mentality!—killed the Professor by sheer will force. Dr. Soone, the blackguard, took sides with the Intelligence, and they both vanished into the fourth dimension, which dimension the Intelligence thoroughly comprehends, whereas even our most brilliant scientists can only theorize upon it. After that, I found myself accused of the murder of Ross."

"But, Dave, how on earth did you extricate yourself from such a ghastly position?" the girl asked in wonder.

"I didn't. I was extricated by a pathologist, whom I never heard of before—Dr. Casby by name. He, by some extraordinary process of speech and production of evidence, proved I was not guilty of the crime. You see, Nan, that pathologist was—hypnotized!"

"Hypnotized!"

"Exactly. He had no conception of what he was saying or doing; he was a tool in the hands of some astounding willpower; he just spoke and acted as that unknown will commanded. It saved my life, anyhow, and I can only think that the Intelligence was the power behind it all. Though why he should try to save me I don't know."

"It's all very peculiar," the girl said pensively. "As you say, it is strange that the Intelligence should desire to save you. . . . Dave, I'm afraid you've done something that is liable to endanger the whole world."

"I know that, but . . . Oh, if only I'd taken your advice!"

"Well, you didn't, and I suppose that is all there is to it. The point is, how do you propose to set about putting an end to this Intelligence?"

"I have no idea—not the vaguest idea. You see, Nan, this creature is so supernaturally clever that it will know all my plans almost before I can think of them myself! The more I dwell on the problem, the more puzzled I become. I can't conceive any way out."

"You can't locate him, then kill him?"

Dave smiled faintly. "About as easy as telling the sun to stop shining," he answered quietly.

There was silence for a moment. The two sat looking at the supper table under the bright light, feeling very much akin to two helpless human beings against the rest of the whole world.

"Is it not rather odd, Dave, that the world has had no manifestation of this creature's power?" the girl asked presently, looking up. "Many weeks have passed since he disappeared."

"I've thought of that myself," Dave responded, with a knit-

[22]

ting of his brows. "Still, I think we can take it for granted that disaster is coming. We have no way of discovering how that monster brain will act, or what steps he will take to gain control over the world."

"True." The girl sank her chin on her cupped hand, then after another long spell of thought she shrugged her shoulders a little hopelessly and looked up into the perplexed young scientist's face. "Never mind, Dave," she said, laying an affectionate hand on his arm. "It's no use blaming yourself. You didn't know what it was going to mean when you made this Intelligence. At heart your motives were for the best. If this creature starts something, we'll find a way to overcome it—never fear!"

"Yes . . . perhaps," Dave assented, but his voice bespoke an inner conviction of infinite futility.

CHAPTER IV   *In New London*

DAVE and Nancy Conisbery had almost dared to hope that some mishap or other had befallen the Intelligence when two years elapsed without a single untoward event. . . . Those first fears had by this time become, to some extent, allayed. Concise reasoning had supplanted that strange sense of horror at the contemplation of the devilish brain that had been loosed upon an unsuspecting world. . . .

The two years had been busy ones for Dave and Nan. Busy—yet futile. All attempts to invent a method of locating and destroying the Intelligence had ended in stubborn and absolute failure. That monster intellect, if still in existence, was machine-proof, detector-proof, ray-proof—proof against everything apparently. . . .

During this period, struggle, disappointments, transient successes, and crushing failures, had changed Dave from the somewhat boyish scientist into a man of mature reasoning, keen perception, and indomitable courage. Together with Nan—now his wife, for they had married in the summer following their reunion—he battled desperately day by day to find some means or system by which his own invention could be located and destroyed. . . .

On June 8th, 2040, a little over two years after the disappearance of the Intelligence—the first evidences of something unusual in the world obtruded itself through the pointless, senseless chaos of a dozen nations' politics and international relationships. Oddly enough, it was the sudden remarkably sensible behaviour of the world's government chiefs, that was considered so unusual. For a reason which remained consistently obscure, and which none of the chiefs seemed willing —or able—to explain, a great conference was held at the Government House, which had its location in Central London. From all countries of the world came a stream of ambassadors and representatives, and the outcome of the conference, notable for its extraordinary brevity, was a declaration of world peace, complete disarmament of every country, sworn oaths that international trade should incontinently follow, the removal of bans, of excessive duties, and of archaic militant debts—the absolute solution of all the childish irritations and restrictions which formerly had formed the greatest barrier to world peace.

The inhabitants of every nation listened to this edict with mixed feelings. As usual there was that element of unrest, but as it existed only in the minority it was rapidly smothered under the rising tide of hope and enthusiasm which seized every country in a remarkably short space of time. . . . All this astounding upheaval and complete alteration in the world's laws occurred in June. By the end of July—in a torrid, insufferably hot summer—half a dozen of the world's greatest nations had agreed, without the least protest, to the institution of one ruler for all the countries—a virtual emperor of the earth. Japan, England, America, Australia, China, and even mighty Russia, all acceded to this new innovation without question.

The world looked on and wondered. The astounding lack of technicalities was literally too good to be true. Utopia seemed actually to hold a chance of resolving into actuality. . . .

The middle of August found the entire world in complete agreement with the election of a world-ruler. Everybody considered that it would be better to unite every land and for all to work for the one purpose. The institution of universal language was mooted. . . .

Then, in the last week of August, when something of the hectic social and political onrush had slowed down, a being of amazing personality arose from the masses—a personality with such incredible control that none dared stand in the way. With infinite calmness this creature picked out two thousand of the world's ablest men in their own particular branches of life— building, soldiering, shipping, engineering, and so on. Nobody ever actually saw this strange being; a perfectly normal man did all the work under his orders—normal, but extremely clever —a doctor-surgeon, some believed.

With a phenomenal helplessness the inhabitants of the world obeyed every command this being saw fit to issue. True, there was a struggle to overthrow the creature. Two hundred of the most intellectual minds of the world trained their brains *en masse* against this creature to overcome its mass-hypnotic power.

The result was astounding. Two hundred insane men were admitted to various asylums, hopelessly deranged.

There was no defying the monster who had risen up. Too late the peoples realized that their respective leaders had been completely hypnotized into their recent strange behaviour. They had agreed to institute a world-ruler against their own wills. To undo all that work was impossible now. The creature had full and absolute control, and could enforce its will in every and any direction. . . .

The consequent enormous changes which followed in the winter months transformed the earth's face completely. Gone were all the stately buildings and artistic streets which had formerly dominated almost every country. In their places were mighty pinnacles and spires of steel structures, all of uniform height, windows piercing their façades from summit to base. These edifices covered almost every country on earth. To have built them by the old system would have taken generations, but by the special machinery invented by the now undisputed Emperor of the Earth, the materials were formed synthetically, and the buildings reared up by mechanical processes within an hour, requiring only one highly trained mechanic to supervise the enormous quantity of intensely complicated mechanism. It was the triumph of machinery.

The institution of a world-language had been rapid, and with it had come the complete stoppage of all former business systems. Food and drink was provided by each country for its own uses and provided for the masses at given times. Money there was none ; wages had ceased, but work went on. Names, too, had been supplanted by numbers and letters, whilst uniforms had been provided for every being on the earth. In accordance with the wearer's position the uniform was a little more or less elaborate. Among the Chosen Two Thousand the uniforms were richly decorated with the Ensign of World Control. . . . The masses had little cause for complaint. They were well treated and well cared for, but their constant work and the loss of their former liberty slowly fanned that underlying spirit of rebellion. Yet there were none who could stand against this monster who had relentlessly instituted all these new laws. . . .

It was with feelings of awe and considerable apprehension that Dave and his wife came to view the world's condition in June, 2041. So far, thanks to an underground home and laboratory, they had avoided capture by the emissaries of the Intelligence, who, day by day, rounded up the few scattered "Old Worlders" in the outlying areas of the countryside. . . .

"There's no denying that the Intelligence has gained control now," Dave remarked grimly. "Looks to me as though we are slowly getting cornered, Nan."

The girl mused for a moment. She looked pensively around the laboratory, where for two years and more she and Dave had fought futilely to devise a means of destroying the all-powerful Intelligence. The countless instruments, the televisor, the ray machine, the thought-vibrator—her eyes travelled over them quickly and a little hopelessly. Finally she shrugged her shoulders.

"After all, Dave, we've exhausted every means we can devise from this lab," she said quietly. "Perhaps it might be better to let ourselves be captured and go into one of the cities. We might find a way there to defeat this colossus."

"Not an earthly way, old girl," Dave responded. "Surely you know how little chance a worker has of getting at the fountain-head? You've seen that from the televisor—and heard it, too."

"The ordinary worker, yes. But we have the advantage of knowing what the Intelligence is, how he was created, and so forth. I'm sure we'd stand a chance," she added with conviction.

"A chance in ten million," Dave responded bitterly. "How many more times must I say, Nan, that the Intelligence knows our moves without the least effort? We're like two new-born babies in the hands of an Einstein magnified to the nth degree."

"You under-rate me, Dave. I know what we're up against—every bit as clearly as you do. I look at it this way. We cannot do any more from this laboratory—we must put our fates in the lap of the gods and try and succeed by outside methods. We may win, or we may fail—I can't say, of course. One thing is quite clear—the world is in a terrible condition; this iron rule cannot be allowed to continue."

"In some ways, I'm inclined to think the Intelligence has done the world a lot of good," Dave said thoughtfully. "All those tomfool restrictions and governmental idiosyncrasies have been finished with—all international jealousy and its attendant vices of hostility and selfishness have been destroyed. There is no unemployment—every man and woman is a unit in one colossal machine-like system, but what that system is, or what it aims at, I don't know as yet. It is inconceivable that the insatiable Intelligence is so easily satisfied. . . . On the whole, though, I really do think—in fact I'm sure—that the Intelligence has made a darn sight better job of controlling than our former country governments ever knew how to."

" 'Knew how to' is about correct," Nan smiled. "The Intelligence is overpoweringly clever—no wonder he has such amazing powers of organization and foresight. Our former rulers never had that, remember."

"I haven't overlooked it, old girl, but I think that any strong man of normally good intelligence could have done all that the Intelligence has done. . . . The Intelligence is too clever to merely finish at such a childish triumph as entire control of the earth."

"You agree, though, that such a state of affairs ought to cease?" the girl asked anxiously. "Think of the coming age—the children. How terrible it is going to be . . ."

"I know." Dave's face was sombre. "Perhaps it's because we're so used to our old way of doing things that this innovation——"

"It's not *natural*, Dave, and you know it!" Nan declared flatly. "We're not being controlled by a clever human being—that wouldn't be so bad—but by an inhuman, sexless devil, uncannily clever, but really only a machine . . . impartial, implacable, deadly! We've got to stop it—somehow!"

Dave did not answer. He sank down into a chair and became lost in moody speculations, his forgotten pipe between his clenched teeth. Nan waited for a while for him to speak, then as he continued to meditate she wandered across to the instrument bench and switched on the televisor.

". . . news from the Central Transmitting Stations of the world, operating on a wave-length of two thousand metres, with a power of two hundred and eighty kilowatts. . . ."

The clear voice of the announcer paused for a moment, and in the televisor the girl saw him look down at his papers. They rustled sharply in the sound apparatus like crackling cinders. Presently he looked up again; his face seemed oddly perturbed, but his voice was steady and quaverless.

"Further orders have been issued today by the Intelligence, acclaimed Emperor of the Earth. These orders are that no

[27]

marriage shall take place as from today; violation of the law will incur the death penalty. The number of workers in the controlling city of New London are to be increased from four million to eight million, and those who are not workers are warned to stand by for inspection by the recruiting forces. The Intelligence announces that sub-atomic air machines and air-liners will henceforth replace our earlier aircraft; all ships have been sunk as useless; all railways destroyed. The Intelligence has proclaimed that dominance and speed can only come by the air. The workers have now completed the twenty-eight thousandth air machine, but as thousands more are needed the workers will have to be doubled. The Central Transmitting Stations of the world are now closing down."

The apparatus became dead. Half mechanically Nan switched off and turned to look at Dave. He was on his feet, his fists clenched, eyes staring glitteringly at the black televisor screen.

"The damned swine!" he breathed at last, looking at the girl. "You heard that first order, Nan?"

"You mean the ban on all marriage?"

"Yes. Don't you see his idea? He aims at creating synthetic beings like himself, gigantically intelligent, until at last we ordinary human beings will be swept off the earth! If we can't even match our brains against one, how on earth are we going to compete against an army of them? Good God! It's destroying the very law of life!"

The girl stood silent. Dave paced about fiercely, drawing at his extinguished pipe. Before his eyes rose a vision of mighty ships sinking with ruthless steadiness in deep waters, of great trains rushing to destruction and ruin, ending in hills of dull red that glowed and winked like sombre eyes, viewing, as it seemed, this new era with kindled hate.

"Well?"

The question came from Nan and penetrated through Dave's absorption. He looked up at her with a start.

"This settles it, Nan!" he said grimly. "We've just got to adopt your idea and go out into the army of workers to try and get at this monster. Somehow—in any way—we've got to stop this business before it goes too far." He stopped and looked around fondly at his instruments. "I hate leaving these," he confessed simply.

"Good heavens, Dave, do be practical! What on earth do these instruments matter when the very livelihood of humanity depends upon your brains?"

"And yours," Dave added quietly.

[28]

Nan smiled slightly. "No, Dave, it's your brains. I can only help. I'm not gifted with your scientific genius."

She stopped perforce as Dave suddenly swept her up in his arms. "And I love you all the better for that," he said softly. "At times I get rather brusque, I'm afraid, but you know I don't mean it. If you were scientific as well, I couldn't love you so much. I often wonder how you can love me . . ."

"I don't love the science in you, Dave—it is *you*," she answered slowly; then with a sudden return to her normal practicality: "Dave Elton, put me down at once. This is no time for love-making. You can do all that . . . later."

Dave lowered her to the floor again and smiled rather like a naughty schoolboy. Then as his eyes happened to alight upon the televisor his jaw suddenly became square, and his face cold and hard.

"We'll go today, Nan," he said. "On foot—to the city of New London!"

*   *   *   *   *

By three o'clock in the afternoon the two were on their way, their underground residence having been safely locked and sealed, should the fates be lenient enough to permit their returning to the laboratory. . . .

There was no direct way from their home to New London, which lay roughly four miles away. The only method was across the moors, through a wood, and so over a hill to the city itself, which lay in the valley beyond.

The two took no provisions or supplies, for it was certain they would reach New London in an hour or two at the most. . . .

The day was one of singular magnificence. Overhead the sky was turquoise blue, brilliant Italian blue, in which was set the brilliant sun. Its blazing heat poured down upon the young man and woman almost pitilessly, cutting their shadows sharp and decisive against the springy green grass. . . . For a long time they went on silently, until the short, fine grass of the moor gave place to a tangled wilderness of long, sharp blades that reached to their knees—the first outcroppings of the wood through which they must pass. In the shade of the massive, foliage-redundant trees they paused for a while, grateful for the coolness and shadow.

Dave removed his coat and spread it upon the grass, then when he and Nan were seated he spoke, for perhaps the first time since their journey had commenced.

[29]

"Have you noticed, Nan, that since the Intelligence took over control we have had perfect weather, according to seasons?" he asked.

This seemed a curious and interesting sidelight upon the main problem. . . .

"Why, no." Nan looked about her and up at the interlacings of deep blue sky through the trembling leaves. "Now you mention it, though, Dave, I believe you are right. We've had perfect summers, hot and dry, wet autumns, sparkling springs, and cold, raw winters. . . . There seems to be none of that old-time vagary—wet one day, then hot the next, and so on. I wonder why?"

"To tell the truth, Nan, I believe that the Intelligence has some way of controlling the elements—some machine or other, maybe. Even our own scientists have tried to devise a means, so I feel sure our brain-monster would not find the problem difficult. It's curious really how many benefits the Intelligence has bestowed as well as cruelties."

"Nevertheless, the cruelties outnumber the benefits," Nan replied steadily. "It is for that reason that the Intelligence must be destroyed. Do you know, Dave, I somehow have not the slightest compunction at the idea of killing the Intelligence —no more than I would have at wrecking an infernal machine. Queer, isn't it?"

"Not at all," answered Dave promptly. "The normal human being, like you and me, shrinks at the very word 'murder'—we hate to injure or maim anything like ourselves, unless we are fiends—but with a machine we feel no such emotion. The Intelligence is relatively only machine-made; we can feel no emotions towards it, no more regret than viewing scrap iron on a heap. . . . The machine is truly the dry rot of civilization."

A long silence fell, then at a curious crackling sound in the undergrowth Dave looked up sharply. He caught his breath in and gripped the girl's arm. "Nan, look," he said softly. "Sit tight, and don't attempt to move off."

Nan suppressed an exclamation and watched intently as a quartet of men in the official uniform of New London slowly advanced in their direction. Presently they came within three feet.

"Names?" rapped out the leader sharply.

Dave scrambled to his feet hastily and assisted Nan to hers. ·

"Of what consequence are names?" he demanded. "We are just fugitives, pretty well beaten into a corner by now, and willing to enter New London as workers. We can't survive by ourselves any longer."

"Married?" the leader enquired.

"Two years."

"You are exempt, then, from the Intelligence's new law that no marriage shall take place as from today. Names at once!"

"Philip Oakley, and—er—Lena Wood, Mrs. Oakley," Dave replied, a grim look in his eyes.

The man made a note and then looked up. "Forthwith you will become Numbers 7788 and 4365Z respectively," he announced in a mechanical voice. "Bring them along."

Before anything could be done two of the men whipped out instruments resembling electric torches, the brilliant beams from which enveloped Dave and Nan completely. Incontinently they felt as though every vestige of energy had been sapped from them. Their arms were powerless and hung limply at their sides, their legs moved only mechanically.

"This is a new one," Dave remarked to the leader. "What is it?"

"Paralysers—invention of the Intelligence," the man returned laconically. "The rays suspend the activity of the nerves in the upper half of the body, and then slightly deaden the lower half. You can just walk, talk, and hear—but nothing else. If you run, you fall. . . . A full strength beam from these paralysers —kills!" he added meaningly, then turning aside led the way through the undergrowth.

On the way the officials picked up four more fugitives, and towards sunset quite a large party topped the hill which overlooked the city. Here the leader called a halt, and speaking into a portable wireless transmitter he carried on his back, ordered an air-machine to carry the party to the city. The captives were then free to sit down and wait, although the paralysers still retained their effect.

Dave, after glancing at Nan and signalling her to say nothing, gave himself up to surveying the city in the valley below. Nearby, the guards, although still diligent with their paralysers, sprawled down on the grassy bank, overcome by the hard work and the marching in the broiling summer sun. They conversed in low voices. They were anything but brutal fellows—they merely had their work to perform. . . .

Below, New London lay like a city in miniature, the blood-red of the glorious sunset reflecting from the countless lofty towers of gleaming metal. The perfectly straight streets could plainly be distinguished, lit with flood-lights at intervals, for in the lower quarters of the city sunlight had faded into deep twilight. . . . The ruby glow crept slowly from half-way up the towers towards their summits. One by one rows of windows became picked out in yellow lights, appearing at that distance like illuminated strings of jewels. From various points lights sprang up, some immeasurably lofty and bright, others dull, glowing, and set low down. . . . The faint hum of power-colossal floated on the still summer evening air. Not a soul was in sight in any of the countless streets, but within the edifices, Dave knew, teeming hordes sweated and toiled their particular shift. . . . Against the distant skyline the New America and New London air liner swept swiftly down like a light-spotted eagle, mammoth wings aspread, towards the directional radio-control tower. It slid down silently to its landing base, guided safely and unerringly by electrical impulses —yet another astounding creation of the Intelligence.

Presently a low hum crept into the undercurrent of throbbing power from the city. A fast air machine of the new design, wingless, travelling with the velocity of a bullet, swept out of the crimson bars laid in the western sky above the city and shot with almost unbelievable speed towards the hill. Motor softly throbbing, a motor that utilized the stupendous force of pure atomic power, the air machine came softly to rest within ten yards of the waiting party.

The pilot stepped out, and with a slight nod to the officials, assisted them to get the captives on board. Dave and Nan found the numbing power of the paralysers suddenly released as they were helped into the surprisingly large rear chamber of the air machine. It was, in truth, just one large cabin, in the front of which was the pilot's seat and instruments. Springed seats were provided, and into these captors and captives alike sank comfortably.

The pilot screwed up the airlock of the vessel, adjusted his levers, and then without the slightest suggestion of motion, due to the gyroscopically controlled interior of the vessel which kept everything on a level keel, the air-machine leapt upwards and climbed steadily, until once again the rays of the setting sun smote it. . . .

Dave and Nan sat silent and enthralled by this marvel of the air as it hurtled towards the city. It was but a brief journey, but the pilot took a long route to avoid the heavy air traffic just instituted between New London and its neighbouring city New Chester, four hundred miles distant.

As the moments passed the astounding ability of the Intelligence forced itself unbidden upon the minds of Dave and his wife. The machine was a marvel, so amazingly constructed that the safest old-time flyer would be, by comparison, a clumsy, unstable kite!

Far below in the light New London twinkled, slowly coming into clearer view as the journey neared its close and the pilot dived downwards. . . . The rays of the sinking sun vanished, a bright glare swept upwards and caressed the flyer—softly it came to rest on the landing platform beside hundreds of its bullet-like contemporaries.

In another moment Dave and Nan were out on the platform with their fellow-captives. Without a word the officials led them down a subway and into a vast area equipped after the style of a super-lounge. It struck Dave as resembling the largest ballroom he had even seen, multiplied ten times. The walls were so distant as to be almost in perspective.

"Be seated," ordered the leader of the officials. "Food will be sent to you. Afterwards you will sleep. Tomorrow the Intelligence will decide what shall be done with you."

"Well," Dave remarked, sinking into one of the chairs, "what do you make of this, Nan?"

"I don't quite know," she replied musingly. "Very much akin to the custom of fattening the turkey before wringing its neck, I'm afraid."

"I don't think so," remarked a man who constituted one of the members of the party. "I thought we'd be treated like cattle and hurled in a cell—like they do in books, y'know. I've heard all kinds of devilish practices attributed to this Intelligence, but sometimes I wonder if he's so bad after all! He's made a good job of controlling the world, y'know. Deny that, if you can!" And his eyes blazed a challenge.

"He's made a good job of it, yes," agreed another—an amazingly stout, middle-aged woman; "but his laws are all wrong! He has prohibited marriage on the penalty of death. How does he think the population is going to grow, I wonder?"

Dave realized here for the first time how unique was his own and Nan's position. Nobody knew the Intelligence was a synthetic being—they all assumed him to be human, but abnormally clever. He smiled oddly and glanced at Nan, who returned him a knowing look.

"I suggest the plan is only temporary," said he who had first spoken, exuding all the qualities necessary to a chairman. "It is a plan—well, say to lower the population, y'know."

"Perhaps he's even going to create human beings!" commented another one, a stoutish, benevolent old fellow—then he burst into explosive laughter at what he considered was a brilliant example of wit. . . . The middle-aged woman regarded him very sourly and distastefully, the "Chairman" merely grinned, and the last member of the party, a lean, cadaverous man who had not spoken a word all along, merely sank deeper into his chair and gazed into space with a pair of chillingly blue eyes.

"Great Scott!" ejaculated Dave presently, and so startled was his tone that the others looked around expectantly. With one accord their jaws dropped and their eyes stared dazedly.

Five gleaming trays, upon which reposed an ample sufficiency of food and drink, floated into the room. They travelled on the air itself in a long line at first, then they broke up into units and became stationary before each of the captives, at lap-level.

The pale blue eyes of the cadaverous one became almost hunted as he looked under and above the tray and waved his hand in thin air. "Good God, it's positively indecent!" he declared flatly, then shut up like a clam as though he had violated some secret personal law.

"Well, I used to think myself a scientist," Dave murmured, "but this Intelligence has got me flummoxed! How the deuce does the fellow do it? Oh, I *say!*"

He shouted loudly to the leader of the officials as he observed him crossing the vast chamber in the distance. The man turned and advanced.

"You want something?" he asked, not unpleasantly.

"I certainly do. How on earth do these trays stand on air? Dammit, man, even the pressure of knife and fork doesn't move them."

The official smiled faintly. "Invention of the Intelligence, which has now been instituted everywhere," he explained in an off-hand fashion. "In this room countless radio waves are projected, passing through it, and are transmitted from the main transmitting station. In these trays—you will observe their thickness—are minute radio pick-ups, which enable the tray to rest on the radio wave as easily as on solid earth or table. The trays are guided by directional radio beams; an official can see you in here by transmitted television—the transmitter being in the centre of the ceiling—and he guides the trays to the separate individuals. Simple, you see."

"It sounds simple—but even I, as a scientist, fail to comprehend how the Intelligence manages it so successfully," Dave replied.

"The Intelligence is beyond comprehension," the official responded ambiguously, and went on his way.

Dave looked after him for a moment, then he shrugged his broad shoulders and voraciously tackled the meal. For a long time he and Nan replenished in silence, then he muttered in an undertone.

"All these astounding inventions, beyond the understanding of normal people, show what sort of a being we're up against, old girl."

"I've been thinking the same thing. We're going to have our work cut out. From all accounts, the Intelligence is surrounded by such a barrier of intellectuals that nobody can get at him."

"I know." Dave looked sombrely before him for a moment. "Yes, we've got a job on, Nan—a terrific job! Still, I started this ghastly business, so I'm going to finish it!" and his jaw closed with a decisive snap.

"Of course we are!" Nan affirmed bravely, but it was the bravery of the superficial. Stout-hearted, courageous young woman though she undoubtedly was, there was a something in the very air, a chilling machine-like quality, that somehow bespoke all the ruthlessness, the devilishness, and the mechanical, inhuman conceptions of the released Intelligence gigantic. . . .

* * * * *

After an uneventful night in a pleasing room adjoining the "ballroom," Nan and Dave both awoke from a surprisingly deep and healthy sleep to find the taciturn leader of the officials standing by the bedside.

"Dress and eat," he said in his level voice. "After your meal you will be interviewed by the Intelligence's Chief Adviser."

"Sounds healthy," Dave remarked dryly. "All right, Mr. —— What is your name, by the way? Somehow, I really like you!"

"My name was Ashton—but now we have numbers I am FW46, and leader of the Military Forces of New London."

"Splendid. Tell me, Ashton, do you like the present rule?"

"There are some edicts it is impossible to defy," returned the official, with quiet evasiveness, and silently departed.

"I like that chap," Dave murmured to Nan. "He's all right at heart—not a harsh strain in him."

"I agree there, Dave."

Thirty minutes later the two had concluded a breakfast from

[35]

the floating trays, and a quartet of men under Ashton's guidance presented themselves. Without any comments being made Dave and Nan were seized and tightly, but not fiercely, held. Still in silence they were led down interminable passages and staircases, twisting and twining, until finally they were ushered into a rather small chamber with walls of dead black, and equipped with all manner of odd-looking machinery. Instinctively Nan shrank back against Dave, and he gripped her arm reassuringly.

"Courage, old girl," he murmured.

"Halt!" Ashton commanded, and then silently withdrew. The door closed and clicked ominously. Dave and Nan looked about them in rather fearful wonder, then jumped violently as a figure entered from behind the curtains on the far wall and advanced slowly and deliberately.

"By jove, it's Soone! Dr. Soone!" Dave exclaimed. "Look, Nan!"

"I know. I've seen him already."

"You have both very good eyesight, and a good memory for faces," the Doctor murmured in a low tone, as he paused before them. "You especially, Mrs. Elton, were quick to recognize me; as you have never seen me personally, I presume it must have been from newspaper photographs!" He extended his hand in greeting.

Dave looked at him coldly. "I prefer not to shake hands with you, Dr. Soone! You know why!"

Soone shrugged, and an irritatingly amused light came into his eyes.

"Because, perhaps, you were inadvertently accused of the murder of our early colleague, Professor Ross?"

"Exactly for that reason! And also because you have taken sides with this infernal Intelligence!"

"As to my taking sides, as you so strangely put it, I . . . Well, I knew the wisest move to make! I am now the sole acting official for the Intelligence, almost ruler of the world, Mr. Elton. With regard to the unfortunate affair of Professor Ross, you must not overlook that you were saved from the death sentence—by us!"

"Whom? You?"

"I said 'us.' I mean the Intelligence—at my suggestion."

"So it was the Intelligence who hypnotised that lawyer into proving me not guilty?" Dave asked. "I suspected as much. Why, pray, did you desire to save me? I should imagine I would have been better out of the way."

"On the contrary, Elton, you are far more valuable alive than dead. You are a clever man, and we have hopes of enlisting your services in the cause of world betterment."

"Indeed!" Dave returned bitterly. "Extremely confident of you both I'm sure—a confidence regrettably premature, however."

The Doctor turned and pulled three chairs from behind the curtains.

"Sit down, both of you, I'm going to give you both a chance —if you refuse it . . . Well, that is your own folly."

Dave and Nan sat down and regarded the urbane surgeon with distinct distaste. He seemed, however, perfectly at his ease.

"You were saved, Elton, as I have said, because you can be of service to us. We want a leading scientist to supervise the making of further synthetic men, and you are the very man to do that work."

"What of yourself? You are more expert than I, if it comes to that."

"I have other things to control; you will be in sole charge."

"I see. Well, I might as well tell you here and now that I refuse! I am out to stop the creation of any more of these brain monsters—much less help to make them!"

"A pity," Soone sighed. "You show surprising lack of foresight, Elton. You know what a magnificent positon you could build up for yourself and Mrs. Elton——"

"Just a minute, Soone. How did you know we were married?"

"I have had you under observation quite a time, my dear fellow—but that is beside the point. As I was saying, you will ultimately become the third most influential man in the world— myself above you, and the Intelligence above us all. Yet you refuse it!"

"You commented on my lack of foresight," said Dave grimly. "Let me tell you I have foresight enough to forsee what the making of more Intelligences will mean to Mankind. Are you fool enough to imagine, Soone, that brains surpassing yours will be content to let you stay as second-in-command? Not on your life! When there are several Intelligences they will overrun the earth, and the slow destruction of the entire human race will begin! I'm out to stop that at all costs."

The Doctor's face became hard. "You mean that?"

"Absolutely final!"

"Most extraordinary! It seems we saved you from the rope just for nothing! Your peculiar view that the Intelligence will

[37]

wipe me out amuses me. I hold such an iron position, they cannot shift me. I know—and I alone—how to make those brains link up to produce such astounding ability. True, the Intelligence could beat me to it easily, but he prefers to rely on me and trusts me implicitly to create beings as intellectually mighty as he is himself. You can see, Elton, I am as near safe as can be! Come now, one last chance, Elton. Will you throw up this positively ridiculous and futile idea of yours to help a doomed humanity—or am I to go through the usual process meted out to a condemned prisoner."

"Go to the devil!"

"It is you who will go to the devil, Elton—you and your wife," Soone returned, his voice cold and metallic. "No, don't get up! Mrs. Elton, come here!"

The Doctor had risen to his feet and was standing before one of the many instruments, his hands on a button.

"What are you going to do?" Dave demanded, jumping to his feet and shielding the girl with his own form. "Get busy on me if you want to, but leave my wife out of this! Just try getting busy on me! I'll give you something for your trouble!"

Soone smiled coldly and looked round significantly. Dave gave a start as he beheld two massive officials standing before the curtains, paralysers ready for action.

"There is nothing to fear," Soone said in level tones. "You have both to go through the same thing. Briefly, every fact and detail of anything you have done or are going to do has to be reflected into this mechanism, which in turn electrically records these impressions on a copper strip—much the same as the gramophone record takes the human voice. Afterwards, these strips will be given to the Intelligence, who will make use of whatever information he thinks useful. The brains of you and your wife no doubt contain many interesting facts—far more so than those of most prisoners. Now, Mrs. Elton, come here. You will not be hurt."

Slowly and reluctantly the girl rose to her feet. Dave made to join her, but the powerful ray of a paralyser held him rigid. He could only fume and glare balefully at the smooth-tongued surgeon. . . . Hesitantly Nan moved towards the complicated mechanism, and Soone silently motioned to the stool in front of it. She seated herself, and with an effort stifled a cry as she felt a magnetic force hold her immovable to the seat. She could not move so much as her finger or her eyes. She sat staring into the tiny black screen of the amazing instrument as though struck with sudden catalepsy.

Dave strained futilely to throw off the power of the paralyser beam. Failing, he sat staring and breathing hard.

"She will not be harmed in the slightest," Soone assured him, and turning pressed the releasing button on the machine. . . .

A thin hum, irritatingly uniform, instantly made itself heard. Two tubes on the top of the machine glowed deep red; the thin whirring sound of the speeding copper tape faintly sounded through the humming. Presently a ray of pale yellow completely enveloped the girl's head, clinging round her fair hair like a halo. She still sat as though carved in stone, staring into the now bright square before her. Her sensations were unfathomable, but most certainly painless. It seemed as though something was singing in her ears, and a vast pressure weighed upon her forehead like a constricting band. . . .

Seconds crept into minutes, and still the speeding tape span on its spools, recording all the knowledge and thoughts she possessed, probing, discovering, merciless. The sense of oppression in her head grew stronger, her breath felt curiously choked. . . That thin infernal hum! It was maddening! And this singing in her ears. . . . Abruptly all went dark before her. . . .

Soone snapped off the instrument and the magnetizer. The girl sagged forward, slumped off the stool, and collapsed in a huddled heap on the floor.

"Fainted," he said laconically. "Anyhow, all the information has been taken from her. She'll soon recover. Put her in her chair there, you two."

Putting down their paralysers so the beams still played upon Dave, the two advanced to the girl. Seizing her unceremoniously by her arms, between them they dragged her to the chair and dropped her into it. Even as they did so she began to reveal the first signs of returning consciousness.

Without any pause Dave was subjected to the same ruthless searching by the machine, but by a supreme effort of will he prevented himself from collapsing under the tremendous strain. When he got off the stool he was shaky and trembling, still in full possession of all he had ever known, but bitterly conscious of the fact that the speeding copper tape had already recorded everything for the Intelligence to view.

"Nan!" he panted, dropping by the girl's side. "Are you better?"

"I'm—I'm all right now," she replied a little uncertainly, straightening up. "I fainted—like the weak little fool I am!"

"There's no disgrace in that. I nearly did the same thing. Are you hurt?"

"Of course not. I only feel—— Feel very tired."

Dave helped her to her feet.

"That tiredness will wear off," Soone remarked indifferently. "It is caused by the strain on the nerves. You'll both be normal within an hour at the outside."

"I hope all you learn does you some good!" Dave grated.

"The Intelligence will make use of all he needs," Soone replied unmovedly. "You two are now workers—dwell on that! You have thrown away all your other chances. You know your numbers, and I have made arrangements for you both to be attached to the air machine factory. There you will assist in sorting out the ores in the refinery and helping to load them into trucks. I hope you will find ample opportunity to help humanity!"

Dave did not answer. He and Nan were seized by the two guards, rendered helpless with paralysers, and led through another confusing maze of seemingly endless passages.

FOR nearly two weeks Dave and Nan toiled at their daily shift in the Factory for Metal Refinement without making any attempts to escape. They had been permitted to work together, as husband and wife, and this at least was fortunate in case any chance of making a fresh move should come along. Their shift lasted from seven in the morning until seven in the evening, allowing thirty-minute intervals for three meals. After seven p.m. they were permitted to go to their own quarters—neat, not unpleasant little quarters in the special section of the colossal city assigned to the workers. . . . At first the work was crushing and arduous, but after three days their muscles became adapted to it. Both were young and phenomenally healthy, so ill effects took on rarity. Rather it hardened them. The overseer, Kelby, was a good man at his work, and not brutal. He possessed a keen sense of justice, and although permitting no lazing, countenanced, by the same token, no working of the unfit or fatigued. . . . On the whole, therefore, the workers were not badly treated.

Yet the thought of being controlled by something or somebody much cleverer than themselves slowly breeded that sense of vivid jealousy—a jealousy flavoured with bitter hatred at the enigmatic fashion in which the unknown Emperor of the Earth had gained his end. There was more than a little hint of rebellion sweeping already amongst the less prescient of the workers. Dave encountered it frequently, and did all in his power to check the flame that smouldered so dangerously. The last thing he wanted was a rebellion; it would only precipitate matters, and in any case result in a complete victory for the mighty Intelligence. That being was unbeatable!

At the commencement of the third week Dave began to grow restless. There seemed to be no outlet for his ingenuity, no chance of exerting his powers in this city so closely guarded and watched. Plans he had made by the score and cast aside as useless; ideas he constantly revolved in his mind, only to bring them to maturity with an absolutely pointless conclusion.

"Undoubtedly my brains are made of sawdust, old girl," he said frankly, as he and Nan worked side by side, sorting out the ores which were slowly conveyed down the chute in front of them to a waiting truck underground—and thence to the refinery. . . .

The girl was silent for a moment, then she muttered in a low voice: "Do you know, Dave, I believe the escape we want is staring us in the face? Has been ever since we came here!"

"Staring us in the face! What do you mean?" Dave spoke to the ores in front of him, for the eyes of Kelby were upon him.

"The chute!"

"The what?"

"The chute. Slide down the chute into a truck below!"

"Good Lord, it's impossible. We might kill ourselves. . . ."

"Why should we? It's only a twelve-foot slide into the truck —then we can bury ourselves under the ores on the truck until the search is given up. After that we're free to move about and try and find a way out of this place we're in."

"I wonder . . ." Dave looked at the chute before him. Certainly the chute was wide enough to admit of a human body. "Nan, it's the simplicity of the thing that might do it," he murmured. "I'll give the word. When I do, dive into that chute like lightning!"

"Right! I'm ready!"

Nearly half an hour passed before Kelby finally moved aside and strolled towards the other end of the edifice. . . .

"Right!" Dave breathed tensely—and incontinently dropping her work, Nan jumped forward to the chute and dived head first into it, to immediately vanish from sight. Without hesitating a second, conscious of a slowly rising uproar about him and

[41]

shouts of alarm and consternation, Dave dived in after her. Followed a giddy rush through total darkness, a fall through a yellow-lit nothingness, and a harsh impact with something hard. Dazedly he looked about him and found, as had been calculated, that he was lying in the truck directly under the chute—a truck three-quarters full of ores.

"Nan!" he whispered hoarsely, and the girl's head lifted above the chippings of metal.

"Bury yourself—quick!" she whispered, and within a few moments the truck was apparently devoid of anything save ores. The two only permitted themselves the tiniest little channel for air, and lay there in that super-heated yellow-lit gloom, perspiring and fearful. . . .

Two underground workers, controllers of the trucks, hearing the slight commotion, presently came and investigated, but never once glanced under the ores in the truck. The startling possibility of two fugitives being beneath them never once occurred to them.

After a time Kelby arrived on the scene, accompanied by two guards.

"Any sign of two workers from the factory 'round here, 29?" he demanded. "They jumped down the chute. Must be somewhere about."

"Not seen them, Kelby," 29 returned. "I heard a noise—but no sign of anybody. What were they like?"

"Young man, strongly built Saxon—and a young woman, his wife. Both fair, and both very athletic. If you find them, nail them. I'll have a look round!"

Tensely Dave and Nan listened to the footsteps of the overseer and his men as they poked about in the dark, gloomy recesses of the underground room. Kelby even stood on the truck and disturbed the surface pieces. Then he dismounted with a grunt of annoyance.

"Clean away!" he snapped. "This is damned serious! It was a neat piece of work that diving down the chute. They've got to be found, though. Come on, we'll send search-parties round about, and leave 29 to keep on the watch down here. Ahoy, there, 29!" he bawled. "Keep your eyes open for those two!"

"Rely on me, Kelby."

"I will."

The heavy footsteps of the overseer receded crunching into the distance. . . .

Even so, the two under the ores dared not move for fear of

[42]

being seen. Showers of ores presently came down the chute as before, and piled on top of them. They managed somehow to keep on obtaining air, but so terrific was the natural heat of the underground tunnel, and their cramped, unventilated place, that they became in time almost stifled. It became obvious that before long a move of some kind would have to be made. . . .

Then footsteps came towards the truck. Following a grinding sound as another truck came along the little trolley-line and took the place of the loaded one. The engineer dispassionately removed the brakes from the loaded truck, and it slowly moved down the incline.

"Good heavens!" Dave choked in a hoarse undertone. "He's set the thing going! Nan, they tip these ores into the furnace for refining!"

Flinging aside all caution he projected his head through the metal chippings, and a second later Nan's face rose also, oddly smudged with grey dust and perspiration. She looked about her.

On both sides the walls of the tunnel were speeding past with appalling quickness, wet and glistening. The truck creaked and trembled as it turned corners and twisted on its way through the dim-lit gloom toward the furnaces.

Dave looked to either side of him in desperation. There was no chance of jumping out: the walls were too close for one thing, and the truck was moving too fast for another. He gazed dazedly at the long chain behind, used for redrawing the truck when emptied.

"Good God!" he muttered, passing his tongue over his lips. "We're in a thorough mess now, old girl. What on earth are we to do?"

"Jump! Better break our legs than get pitched into the fire!"

"We'll kill ourselves jumping off at this rate, Nan! We'll have to hang on for a while, and jump for it, if the worst comes to the worst."

The truck moved faster and faster, carried by its load and the steep tilt of the tunnel floor. . . . At length it rounded yet another bend, and far ahead the two beheld the red glow which they knew came from the furnaces. Here, one man alone did the work. Mechanical devices alone toiled—vast arms of metal-controlled colossal cauldrons and crucibles, switches and buttons actuated the machinery which sifted pure metal from impure—one man alone in a cool box jammed with apparatus controlled the metal monster which was fed with the life-blood of the mammoth refinery. . . .

Horror on their faces, Dave and Nan stared ahead as the truck careered down the remaining slope.

"Look!" Nan shouted abruptly. ·"It stops there—tips over and throws its load into the fire—then comes back up the other line——"

The truck went on relentlessly.

"That chain and girder there—just beyond the edge!" Dave bawled hoarsely. "See it? Jump for that! Last chance——"

The two clambered over the side of the swaying truck and clung on tenaciously. But six feet to the end of the line, then—— They leapt, madly and blindly, across the gap to the mighty chain which hung down into the seething, boiling furnace below.

With clutching fingers Dave clawed at the heavy links, swinging like a pendulum in mid-air. He gave a shout. Nan was just above him, clinging with one hand, twisting from side to side. Her frenzied voice came down to him.

"Dave! I can't hold! I'm falling——"

She twisted further round, and Dave clutched his own link with one bent arm. He flung out his other arm and braced himself for a sudden shock. . . . Nan screamed and suddenly dropped from the link above, but immediately the arm of Dave crushed around her waist and dragged her to him. "Grab hold! Quick!" he panted. "Hurry! You're a weight!"

Her hands seized the link fiercely and Dave relaxed his grip with a low sigh of relief. . . .

Ghastly, sickening waves of heat came beating upwards, with clouds of acrid, choking smoke. Below—far below—the white-hot sea of the molten metal boiled and bubbled turgidly. . . .

Slowly, shakily, Nan crawled painfully up the remaining length of chain to the top, and at last scrambled out on the great girder, from which the chain depended. Fixing herself so she could not possibly fall, she paused and extended a hand to Dave. ·

"Gosh! That was close!" he breathed, as he came up beside her.

"I thought I was finished!" Nan spoke tremulously, and a short breathless laugh escaped her. She looked downwards into the seething murk far below. "What now?" she asked.

"Carry on," Dave responded, and commenced to worm his way, little by little, along the gigantic girder which formed the arm of this crane-like machine. Presently he came to the vertical support with its foot-holds and began to descend carefully.. The task was not difficult, and very shortly he and Nan were together on the concrete floor.

[44]

To their rear was the metal-pit; before them, another tunnel-opening.

Dave ruminated. "The underground resources of this city are pretty vast, and I've no idea what we may run into. The only thing to do, old girl, is to carry on until we finally come to the surface. If we ever get there, we can lay other plans. If anybody comes along we shall have to do our best to hide. Come on. We've got no lights, so we'll have to trust to our sense of touch."

"I'm ready if you are. Lead on. Anything's better than just stopping here."

They advanced slowly, and within a minute the blackness of the near-by tunnel had swallowed them up. Ahead there was not even a hint of light, and behind only the dull reflected glow from the metal-pit served to provide a faint illumination. In time, however, this too faded, and complete blackness descended. From a seemingly vast distance, smothered and heavy with the intervention of solid earth, came the throb of New London's factories. In some curious way, it was comforting: it helped to maintain a grip on earthly and mundane things. . . .

Time passed, and fatigue and reaction began to slowly assert themselves. Nan walked with dragging footsteps, and Dave hardly a whit the better.

"We've got to go on, old girl," he breathed, seizing her arm and striving vainly to see her face in the ebony darkness. "We can't stop here, and the tunnel can't last for ever. It leads to the open somewhere. The very draught of fresh air proves that. . . ."

The girl said nothing, and the plodding advance continued. After perhaps ten minutes Dave stopped abruptly. "Look ahead, Nan. Light! Yellow light! Go cautiously."

Hope renewed, fatigue was to some extent allayed. Withal, care was exercised to its limit, and with noiseless swiftness the two sped onwards, quickly now, thankful to be able to use their eyes again and escape from the impenetrable blackness. Again Dave stopped, and he and Nan looked at each other with startled eyes, as a series of screams and shouts came floating from the lighted square ahead. Quite suddenly the din formed itself into a string of husky oaths, the crack of a whip-lash, and a high-pitched voice shouting with pain.

"There's some foul work or other going on there!" Dave muttered, clenching his fists. "Come on!"

"But Dave, think of——" Nan shrugged her shoulders hopelessly as Dave unheedingly tore up the remaining stretch of

[45]

passage as fast as his legs would take him. At a run she followed him, and then stopped involuntarily at the entrance of another underground work-shop at the sight she beheld.

Close to a machine an old man, somewhat bent and obviously of no great physical strength, was crouching vainly from the slashing blows of a vicious whip. Wielding the whip was a powerful fellow with gleaming bare shoulders and immensely muscular arms. A revolting profile, with flattened nose and prognathous jaw, was silhouetted against the yellow light in the roof.

"So you thought you'd escape, huh?" the man demanded, pausing for a moment. "Let me tell you this, you old fool! No man ever escapes from this underground workshop—ever! See? And here's a bit more of the lash to teach you——"

"That's where you're wrong!" snapped Dave, leaping forward lightly and clutching the man's wrist.

"Eh? What?" Snatching his hand free the man stood glaring fiercely. "An' who the devil are you, anyway? Another one just trying to escape, eh? Well, take——"

Dave wasted no more time on words. He swung round his right fist with all his strength and dealt the man a terrific blow on the side of his jaw. The surprise nature of the assault took him completely off his guard, and with a foul oath he fell over backwards upon the concrete floor.

"Quick!" Dave panted, jumping forward and seizing the old man by his arm. "We've got to get out of this! Anywhere—anyhow! Are you trying to escape?"

"Yes—yes, and——"

"Never mind that!" Dave jumped forward and knocked over the fellow with the whip as he was about to gain his feet again. "My wife and I—also fugitives," he flung out. "Come on!"

Half carrying the old man between them, Dave and Nan ran down the tunnel on the opposite side of the chamber, floundering ever and again in the darkness and banging themselves against the walls, until finally, as no sound of pursuit made itself heard, Dave called a halt and a rest.

"Thank goodness there are dozens of branch tunnels," he murmured. "There's no way of finding which way we've gone. How are you, sir?" he asked of the old man, as they all three sat down upon the floor.

"All right, thanks to you; only a little out of breath," came the quavering reply from the darkness. "Really, though . . . to whom am I indebted for this act? You saved me from that whip, and have helped me on the way to the freedom I was trying to find alone."

"I'm Worker 7788—and this young lady here whom you saw in the light of the cavern, is my wife—4365Z."

"Never mind numbers. What are your names? We are friends, I—hope? I am Professor Rupert Athlinstone. I am a scientist—or rather, I *was* a scientist, until this accursed monster came to rule the world."

"Indeed, sir?" Dave spoke eagerly. "My name is David Elton; I, too, am a scientist. My wife is named Nancy—Nan for short."

"David Elton. H'm! I seem to have heard your name, young man, in connection with some experiment on the new wireless transmitters at Melthinstowe."

Dave smiled with inward pride in the darkness. "Quite right, Professor. I am the guilty one. I say, though—how extraordinary to meet another scientist! Why, between us—forgive my presumption, sir—we might be able to do something to alter the ghastly mess the world is in. Of course, I don't pretend to be as far advanced in knowledge as you are—I haven't even attained Professorship."

"We're up against a big problem, son," the old scientist replied. "You see, this Intelligence is not a human being—he is nought but the creation of some misguided scientist. I have found that out for myself. Somehow, some scientist has been ingenious enough to find a way to make use of the entire human brain capacity, and has created a synthetic being around it. May that man be cursed to his dying day—if he's not already dead!"

Dave clutched Nan's hand convulsively in the darkness.

"But how can you be sure that the Intelligence is man-made, sir?" he asked tensely.

"I have been employed in the laboratories, son, and close enough at once to see and study the Intelligence himself. He has no emotions at all, no soul, no passionate impulses, cannot laugh or cry, be humorous or despondent. He is just one vast intellect, with a body so flawless and nerveless that he just cannot be a human-begotten human being. He is a laboratory creation. I once worked out a plan of my own how to accomplish so great a feat, but I stayed my hand, because I knew what destruction and disorganization such a being could bring on the world at large. . . . Now some other scientist has done the same thing, without any foresight, and precipitately. The fool! The consummate idiot!"

"What would you say, Professor, if I told you I was the

[47]

man who did it?" Dave asked bitterly.

A sharp gasp of amazement came out of the darkness. "You! Good heavens! Surely—— It's incredible!"

"I'm afraid it's true, sir. I thought of the idea, and——"

"Yes, but did you actually make the creature and release it upon the world?"

"I——" Dave began, then Nan suddenly interjected.

"No, Professor, he did not. He thought of the idea, and waxed enthusiastic over it. He called in two experts, and they made the creature, didn't they, Dave?"

"They did," Dave assented, and proceeded to give an account of the happenings connected with the making of the Intelligence, up to the time of the altered world and his own incarceration in the city of New London.

"I see," said Athlinstone at last in a grim voice; then in a more tolerant tone: "My boy, you were not to blame, don't think that. It was up to your more experienced partners to have seen what such an experiment would mean."

"Professor Ross had his doubts from the outset, sir, but Dr. Soone influenced him."

"I can well credit that," Athlinstone replied in a hard tone. "I have met Soone, and he's nothing more than a smooth-tongued scoundrel, entirely blind to everything save his own ambitions. Brilliantly clever—but underneath it all, a devil! No, son, you were acting in what you thought were the best interests; you were inexperienced and impetuously generous to a very hard and intolerant world. At your age I would have done exactly the same thing. Thank heaven, though, I only had the idea quite recently, when I could first sum up the ways of men, and how they would react to such an innovation. You say your present wife—you of course were then unmarried—tried to dissuade you?"

"Yes. Like a pig-headed idiot I wouldn't listen."

"In any case, son, Soone would have gone on with it, so you have nothing to blame yourself for."

"I am trying to level things out, Professor—right the wrong my own mind virtually conceived."

"You have a plan of some kind?"

"Not the vaguest, yet. Perhaps we might be able to think of something between us, as we're both in the same profession."

"I did have hopes, but unhappily those devils destroyed my workshop at the time they captured me. I have nowhere to work."

"Then—then where were you making for, sir?"

"Anywhere!" the old man returned almost savagely. "Anywhere out of this city, to some place where I can think and view the position! That beast with the whip caught me, and. . . . Well, never mind that! Where were you making for?"

"Like you—for anywhere," Dave replied slowly; "but, do you know, I have an idea. My own laboratory is some two miles from the city and being underground is quite inaccessible to any stranger. What do you say if we try and make for it?—all three of us? I have a good selection of equipment there, and perhaps we'll be able to figure out something. What do you say?"

"It's a wonderful idea, son, and I thank you from the very bottom of my heart. The risk of getting there, though—beyond the city. . . ."

"We'll do it!" Dave interjected confidently. "But we won't if we sit here much longer. There'll be search-parties finding us before long! We'd better get on the move while things are still quiet. Can you last out, sir?—and you, Nan?"

"I am quite prepared," the Professor responded, gaining his feet.

"It's not a case of lasting out," Nan remarked from the darkness; "we've got to go on or give up everything we've gained so far. It's literally a matter of life and death. Carry on, Dave —we're ready."

CHAPTER VI   *The Genius*

LATE evening found the three fugitives at the base of one of the many ventilation shafts of the underground tunnel. All through the afternoon and early evening they had skulked in the deep shadows—for the shaft threw a faint light in the gloom—pressing themselves against the wall in the complete darkness, when anybody happened to pass on his way to the underground workshops. These individuals carried lights, but fortunately they were relatively weak, and being unprepared to find any escaped workers, they took no particular pains to look searchingly about them. Such moments, nevertheless, were tense and fraught with danger, but each time the dense shadows and unwariness of the passer-by saved the three from discovery.

Exhausted though they were from constant suspense, labour, and absence of food, their determination to escape the city at nightfall was no whit abated. . . . As the pale light of after-sunset slowly faded from the sky and the diffused gloom of the summer night advanced, Dave moved from his position and looked up the colossal shaft. A circle set with stars hung far overhead.

"I think we might venture now," he murmured to the others. "All seems quiet above. We'd better risk it. You go first, Nan; you next, Professor, and I'll come last—then if either of you slips, I can save you from falling, perhaps."

Dave lifted the girl up to the first rung of the ladder locked into the wall of the shaft, and she slowly climbed upwards, her heavy boots scraping noisily on the rungs.

"Quietly!" Dave whispered. "For the love of Mike, Nan!"

"Sorry. These boots are so clumsy." She went on steadily.

The Professor, although not particularly agile, managed somehow to advance upwards rung by rung with Dave directly below him, anxiously on the alert for the first sign of a slip. . . . All went well, however, and after a seeming eternity Nan topped the shaft and peered cautiously about her. "All quiet!" she breathed, as the city lay silent on her right hand, work for the day having ceased. On every other side stretched the towering sides of the valley in which the city lay.

With great care, making as little noise as possible, the three climbed the shaft rim and presently stood up together under the stars.

"Good!" Dave murmured in satisfaction. "No signs of pursuit, anyhow. The thing now is to find a way up the valley side and through the woods to my laboratory and home. It's going to be hard going, tired as we are, but there's nothing else for it. We daren't stop a moment if we're to get through."

"Only too true," agreed the Professor. "Let us be going. I can stand more yet."

"What about you, Nan?"

"Don't worry over me, Dave. I'm not made of putty, anyhow."

"Good, old girl. You're a sport. Come on!"

They set off across the short, flat grass of the moor, away from the city, towards the valley side. They reached it without mishap, for there were no city dwellers on these outskirts. The city itself was entirely surrounded by a high wall and guarded at many points, but thanks to the ventilation shafts bringing them up beyond the city the three had escaped all that hazardry. The thought of fugitives using the ventilation shafts as a means of escape had probably never occurred to the officials of New London. There was nothing to live for beyond the city, in any case; all home life had long ceased—only in extreme cases like

[50]

Dave's and the Professor's was escape worth the risk. . . .

The moon was rising, yellow and globular from the purple mists as the three toiled wearily up the valley side. It was a hard and arduous climb, for the way was strewn with small stones and rubble, and in places the inclines were steep and precipitous. By climbing and resting in turn, however, they managed little by little to continue upwards, until at last they topped the edge of the valley and had the spacious moorland before them again. . . . Far below them New London lay a twinkling enormity under the moon, a pool of light-dots, surrounded by the frowning, dark masses of the valley side. Dave looked down at it and smiled a little grimly.

"We've got something on our plate to disorganize all that, and bring the Intelligence himself to destruction, eh, Professor?"

"Indeed we have," the old scientist assented gravely. "Still, we had the brains to make the Intelligence—you in practice, and myself in theory—so surely we ought to have the brains to destroy it! We will devise something with our joint activities. I am confident of it."

Nothing further was said, and the long journey across the moor and through the forest was continued in silence. The woods possessed a strange ghostliness in the moonlight. Once an owl hooted eerily, and somewhere a branch snapped like a rifle shot. Underfoot small branches and dead twigs crackled noisily, no matter how lightly the three trod. Here and there little glades and clearances leapt into phantom-like relief in the moonlight, to be instantly passed as the progress through the inky shadows of the woods continued.

The three were close to the point of exhaustion, when at last the underground home was reached. Dave fumbled wearily with the combination lock, and at last it clicked beneath his aching fingers, cramped and bruised from the climbing and tugging he had undergone in the past twelve hours.

The three passed into the hall, and Dave carefully resealed the door—a door proof against all the acids and explosives in existence. He switched on the light and led the way into the spacious drawing-room. . . .

Despite the curiously deserted air that hung over the place, and the musty smell indicative of long absence, the three sank incontinently into easy-chairs and for a few minutes, at the least, made not the slightest effort to speak or move. Then with a tremendous effort Dave aroused himself.

"I'll go and get something to eat and drink," he said, bending down and switching on the electric fire. "I won't be long."

[51]

Within ten minutes he was back with sandwiches and hot coffee. With typical masculine clumsiness he placed them on the table.

"Come on, Nan—and you too, Professor. Let's have a meal; then we'll be better."

The two wearily drew up to the table and ate with purely perfunctory effort. Half-way through her second sandwich Nan's head was lolling gently to one side ever and again, but with a start and an effort she aroused herself each time.

"Sleepy?" Dave asked gently.

"Sleepy! Never so sleepy in my life before. I—I——" Even as she spoke her sandwich dropped from her fingers to the carpet, and she slumped gently back into her chair, breathing deeply and regularly. Dave grinned and looked at her admiringly.

"She's a wonderful girl, Professor—a girl a chap can be proud to call his wife. She's got grit to the backbone. Excuse me a moment, will you?"

"Why, certainly." The Professor seemed to have transiently revived under the influence of hot coffee and sandwiches. He looked on with a smile as Dave picked the girl up bodily in his arms and carried her carefully to the next room. . . .

"Dead off," Dave remarked, as he returned. "Which reminds me that I'm in no fettle for a ten-mile walk. We must get sleep before we do a thing further. Come with me, sir, and I'll show you your room."

"Thank you, my boy—thank you."

The following morning found all three normal again, in the matter of energy, at least. True, bruises and intense stiffness were the price of the previous day's proceedings, but as time passed these inconveniences wore off. After a hearty breakfast Nan took over the control of the domestic regions with her customary, unobtrusive skill, and Dave and the Professor retired to the laboratory.

Dave had been agreeably surprised at the old fellow's appearance in the daylight, and after a long rest. He seemed less bent and shaky, and his lean face had lost all its former tendency to the cadaverous. He was fairly tall, and somewhat narrow-shouldered. The immense forehead, the keen grey eyes, and square chin bespoke the man of intellectual power, and patient determination in the face of set-backs.

Dave watched his quick, capable hands as he tapped instruments and bottles during his survey of the laboratory. At length he turned and remarked:

"You have a well-equipped laboratory here, son."

"I'm glad to hear you say that, sir." Dave moved forward, hands in pockets. "I've been improving on it for years now, and I flatter myself it pretty well contains everything of use in the chemical and scientific line. . . . And now—please don't think I'm trying to hurry you at all—I would like to know what you propose to do. For every day that the Intelligence is in power the world gets harder and harder to release and to bring back to the normal. We must devise some plan or other, and that very soon. And when we make that plan we must risk our all—to win or lose!"

Athlinstone looked at the young eager face searchingly for a moment, then he smiled paternally. "Good for you, boy! You've got character. Every word you have uttered is correct. Yes, our plan must be sound from beginning to end . . . must be as solid and immovable as New London itself!"

"No small job," Dave muttered. "I confess, for myself, that I have no plan at all yet. Have you?"

"Yes . . . I . . . have," Athlinstone responded, slowly and pensively. Then without another word he seated himself at the table and drew a sheet of paper and a pencil towards him from the rack. For a while he figured apparently, at random and traced concentric circles with the air of an expert; then dropping the pencil very abruptly he sank down into deep thought, from which Dave did not dare arouse him. . . .

At last he spoke.

"Dave, there is only one way to overcome the Intelligence!"

"And that is?" Dave asked eagerly.

"To make something cleverer than himself!" The Professor sat back in his chair and awaited the effect of his statement. He did not appear surprised at Dave's startled expression, or his incredulous voice a moment later.

"But, sir—how on earth are you going to do that? The Intelligence is the quintessence of all that is intellectual. There cannot be anything on the earth cleverer than he!"

"There shall be!" Athlinstone returned grimly. "I have already mentioned to you that I once evolved a formula for the creation of a being almost identical with this one of yours—which is now the Intelligence. But, now we have seen what an uncontrolled, synthetic intellectual monster can do, we must guard against that, and instead make a brain machine which is solely under our control, and which will only do what we want. You follow?"

Dave sat down. "Yes, I quite follow. Tell me, what do you

propose to do?"

"Make a man, not of flesh and blood, but of machinery! In this machine we will install not an actual brain as we know it, but high-powered instruments capable of amplifying our own thoughts to whatever extent we desire. By that means we can always think higher than the Intelligence, and in the end, you can rest assured, machinery will get the better of even the Intelligence's vast intellect. It will take time to build this machine, but when it is finished I am sanguine that we will have the position entirely in our own hands!"

"I see," Dave assented, nodding slowly. "We will amplify our own thoughts, then reflect them, putting them to such uses as we deem fit?"

"Exactly that. You have the equipment here necessary for such a purpose."

For a moment Dave considered, then he thumped the table top decisively. "It's a wonderful idea, sir! About the only one which will work, I should think. We can get busy right away, and——"

"Just a moment, my boy, just a moment," Athlinstone murmured, raising his hand. "There is another thing yet I have to discuss with you; something that will aid us considerably. A mind-directional beam instrument."

Dave stared almost rudely at the old genius. "A what, sir?"

"An instrument which I myself have perfected. Unfortunately, at the time of my capture, it was destroyed along with my laboratory, but as you have all the material here for the building of another one, I can construct it in two days at the outside. This instrument is really an invention for projecting thought vibrations—thoughts send out impulses, as you are aware—and also, my little machine receives them. You see, this instrument of mine works like a wireless transmitter, but, instead of transmitting radio-waves, it transmits thought-waves, and, if a person be supplied with one of my tiny transmitters—and it matters not how far distant he or she may be, since there is no barrier to thought-vibration—the person can send his thoughts through its agency. It matters not where it is on the person; it vibrates perpetually. My receiver picks them up. They are then transformed into their original condition, and projected on a small screen. Of course, the result is a moving picture of whatever is in the person's mind. You see?"

"Wonderful! Wonderful!" Dave breathed. "How, though, do these thoughts travel? What do they travel on?"

"They travel on a beam—an invisible beam—emanated by

the transmitter. That is its secret. The advantage of such an instrument will be that, wherever you may be, you can always communicate with me *via* thought, even if the transmitter is fastened by a cord about your neck and hangs down on your chest. Or, if you are at the receiving end, I can communicate with you. The transmitter is no larger than a cameo brooch. One of the first things I am going to do is to equip ourselves—your wife included of course—with these transmitters, and fix the receiver here in the laboratory. When that is done we will get to work with the Intelligence No. 2—and it is going to be the saviour of the world—not the destroyer!"

"You're right there, sir!" Dave declared heartily. "I begin to think that Heaven itself led you my way yesterday. With your genius, I feel doubly secure. We'll win in the finish—or die fighting!"

"We'll not die," Athlinstone answered quietly, and rising to his feet began to search round for the various components essential to his astonishing device—the mind-directional beam instrument. . . .

*   *   *   *   *

Two days elapsed before Athlinstone's startling invention was completed. Two days of close contact with the old Professor had revealed to Dave that, clever though he himself was, the old man was infinitely cleverer. Had he been a lover of publicity and the limelight—which he certainly was not—Athlinstone could have become the leading scientist of the day in the old order of things. He preferred, however, to keep to himself, and it was perhaps this aloofness from others that promoted the unhindered development of his extraordinary intellectual powers. Subjects which would have been difficult even to a trained scientist seemed like a child's problems to him. If ever a man was fitted mentally to invent a machine to overthrow the Intelligence, Athlinstone was certainly that man!

The completed mind-directional instrument resembled, in effect, a complicated wireless set, possessing a dynamo of its own. The panel was occupied by only three cerebrated dials and a button. On the top of the instrument reposed the tiny ground-glass screen which revealed, in movement and sound, the exact thoughts of the person at the transmitter, whether far or near.

"Dave," the Professor smiled, handing him a small, square object hanging by a black cord, "take this to your wife, ask her to put it around her neck, and tell her then to think of anything she deems fit, and you will see on this screen what the result is."

[55]

"Right, sir."

Dave went off and found his wife working the instrument which created synthetic foods—the wonderful little machine, which had provided food in plenty for over three years, and could go on doing so eternally if necessary. She smiled a trifle sceptically at Dave's request, but nevertheless complied with his wishes.

"Think of anything you like," Dave said once again, and then departed to the laboratory once more. . . .

"Ready?" the Professor inquired, his hand on the switch of his instrument.

"Yes," Dave grinned faintly. "Nan seems to be rather on the dubious side, Professor. Anyhow, she is game enough."

"Sit down, Dave, and watch this little screen." Athlinstone quietly motioned to a chair, and pushed in the switch of the receiver. A hardly distinguishable whirring arose from the generators. Slowly, a suggestion of light crept over the lifeless ground glass face of the "imagor." Followed a sudden pinging sound, resembling the sudden replacement of a telephone receiver upon its hook. . . .

Dave leaned forward and stared at the screen amazedly.

Upon the ground glass plate the figure of Nan became slowly visible, surrounded by the familiar articles of the model kitchen. She appeared to be gazing straight before her, a smile, still slightly sceptical, forming on her lips. Then, quite abruptly she appeared in different surroundings—in a glorious garden, redundant with incredible flowers and foliage. Slanting sunlight was catching the shimmering fairness of her hair. . . . The view faded, then with bewildering rapidity she appeared in strange and unearthly surroundings, time and time again—upon each occasion attired in different clothing, and seeming, by some unexplained process, more lovely with every change. Ordinarily she was not beautiful; hardly even pretty. She possessed keen and practical features and a splendid pair of grey eyes, but her mouth and nose were altogether too disproportionate to permit of even the vaguest claim to beauty.

It was curious to Dave, for this very reason, to observe how these defects were absent in the transmitted image of Nan. From head to foot she was a literal shimmering magnificence—womanhood superb—a glorious girl in glorious environment.

Again came the pinging note. Dave looked up to find Athlinstone smiling somewhat enigmatically.

"Professor, Nan is not, I feel sure, so beautiful as that!" Dave nodded dumbly to the screen, now blank and lifeless. "And those surroundings! They were absolutely unearthly—heavenly! I've never seen anything like them before."

"They were purely the figments of your wife's imagination, Dave. Remember that this machine reflects the thoughts. You saw exactly what was in her mind—she envisioned herself as an ideal woman in ideal surroundings. You saw, in brief, exactly what she thought!"

Dave slowly shook his head and smiled ruefully.

"And to think I considered myself a good scientist!" he remarked, with dry self-condemnation and some envy.

"Needless flattery for me, son," Athlinstone said quietly. "You must not forget that I am nearly thirty-seven years more experienced than you. In thirty-seven years it is quite probable that you will be able to exceed my efforts. . . . Which reminds me, Dave, that the making of this instrument has revealed something else to me—a plane of vibrations are set up by a brain's thoughts; but the action of a negative vibration wave—that is one of sufficiently low frequency to prevent and block these waves—can render us completely proof against anybody's thoughts."

"It sounds good, Professor," Nan remarked, as she came into the room. "Really, sir, you positively ooze ideas. Oh, how did my thoughts go down by the way?" she asked mischievously.

"Perfectly," Dave responded, putting an affectionate arm about her shoulders. "We'll show you the instrument in action a little later on. At the moment I just want to hear about this new idea of the Professor's. Vibrations which can stop a mind probing beyond a certain distance may come in mighty useful as a weapon of defence against the probing Intelligence."

"I cannot discuss it now to any extent, though," the older man remarked, shaking his head. "I have the idea—but I must work it out. I want to make it impenetrable—so that not even the all-powerful Intelligence can break the barrier. It will take time, of course, but when it is complete, along with my mechanical brain-power amplifier, we will be in a position to give the Intelligence what is owing to him."

"We should be," Nan admitted, fingering the black cord at her neck; then, as though it had suddenly taken possession of her thoughts—"Tell me, Professor, am I to keep this little box of an affair upon my person?"

"Certainly, Nan. I have one, and Dave, so you of course must do likewise. If anything ever happens to any of us, the one who is safe can tune in this instrument of mine and tell by the scenes reflected what is taking place in the mind of the absent one. From these scenes we will be able to judge where the missing one is."

Nan laughed oddly. "Supposing, though, the other one did not think?"

"You can never cease to think," the old man replied gravely. "All the time these transmitters round our necks are picking up our thought vibrations, but they are not resolved unless the receiver is switched on—no more than a radio programme can be heard until the set is connected. Yet the waves are still in the aerial. The programme is there . . . unheard; and, in the case of television—unseen."

"I begin to see," the girl murmured thoughtfully. "At any time, then, by switching on your set, you can see exactly what any one of us is thinking? Even if asleep? The subconscious mind is at work even during sleep, is it not? We dream . . ."

"Precisely. Always—until death—your thoughts, your very innermost thoughts, are reflected on the screen—the imagor. And, who knows, even after death, maybe. So," Athlinstone added, with a dry chuckle, "have a care what you think about!"

Nan laughed. "I will. Tell me, though, Professor, how do you know you've got the right person? They'll all come in at once, won't they?"

"Typical of your keen mind, Nan. The answer to your question is 'no.' Each of us have a different mind, of varying strength—or, technically, different frequencies—therefore, these come in at different points of the controlling dial. Similar, in effect to the different metre wave-lengths of wireless stations. On this instrument your number is 52, mine is 16, and Dave's we have yet to place. Come here, both of you, and I'll give you a thorough knowledge of how to work the instrument."

CHAPTER VII   *Escape*

As the weeks passed, and the furious heat of that amazingly dry and glorious summer gave way to the cooler, shorter days of autumn, the amazing genius of Professor Athlinstone gradually expanded itself, to great and hitherto undreamed-of achievements. Having nothing to disturb him, so secure was the underground laboratory, he strained every nerve and fibre in a tremendous effort to complete the invention which he felt sure would overcome the Intelligence.

After the final perfection of his thought-transmitter, he set about an abstruse study of the vibrations which would stop thought-waves from passing. To find the precise vibrations necessary, demanded a considerable amount of experiment with the attendant failures and transient successes, but the old scientist went on doggedly. It was during the struggle to find the elusive vibration, that he stumbled upon that which the Intelligence already thoroughly understood—the fourth dimension. He found the exact mathematical relationship needed to place him in and out of the fourth dimension, and by a machine of infinite complication he did at last manage successfully to transfer himself into the dimension and out again. . . .

This problem mastered—fortituous though its inception had been—he continued with the vibration puzzle, until at length he had progressed far enough to construct a light metal helmet, which by a system of wires carrying the vibrations from a small battery upon the back, prevented outside thoughts from disturbing the wearer's brain. Having thus far succeeded, he struggled resolutely to find a way to use the vibrations over any area—to shield the entire laboratory, if possible.

There was to be no outside interference.

*   *   *   *   *

He was intently studying the problem one early morning when Dave came rushing in, his face agitated and eyes full of alarm.

"Professor, have you seen Nan?" he demanded almost rudely.

Athlinstone looked up from his instruments in surprise.

"Why, no, Dave. What is——"

"She's disappeared!" Dave cut in pantingly. "She was in the bedroom half an hour ago, brushing her hair prior to coming down to breakfast. Now I can't find her. I've looked everywhere . . ." Dave stopped, his face haggard.

"Use the thought-receiver, my boy," the older man counselled quietly. "That will show you everything."

"By Jove, yes!"

Dave sprang across to the instruments and twisted the dial No. 52. Switching on the generators, he gazed intently at the ground-glass screen. . . . For a flashing instant he caught a glimpse of New London, mighty and invincible in the rosy dawn—then came a view of Nan herself. She was standing in a small cupboard-like affair, with steel bands gripping her body in a ruthless firmness. Her grey eyes were wide open, unusually wide and staring, and her mouth and chin set hard. Dave gasped a little as he beheld drops of perspiration on her brow, which began presently to trickle down her set, white face. She seemed to be undergoing some titanic mental conflict. . . .

By degrees the view changed and the figure of the Intelligence himself, Dr. Soone, and several strangers came into being, still and intent. . . .

Then blackness. . . . The scene vanished and the screen became blank. Frantically Dave twisted the controls of the instrument—then suddenly he felt the Professor's restraining hand upon his arm. The old scientist's face was as set as granite, and the keen grey eyes were cold.

"No use doing that, son," he said, shaking his head.

"But, sir—— The Intelligence! That damnable, filthy creature has got Nan somehow, and——"

"I know. I saw it all," Athlinstone answered. "Nan is in the clutches of the Intelligence, and for some reason or other she has lost consciousness—fainted, maybe. That is why we cannot get her thoughts."

Dave clenched his fists. "I'm going after her!" he rapped out savagely. "What's more, I'm going to blow up the whole vile bunch! Give me some fulminate of mercury, Professor. That'll blow the lot of them to Hades!"

"Yes—and Nan as well," came the steady answer. "And you! Good heavens, Dave, what are you thinking of? Fulminate of mercury would wreck the city! No, you had better wear one of my thought-proof helmets, and take one with you for Nan. If you can rescue her—which may God grant!—you will both be proof against any thought influence the Intelligence can devise. I would come, too, but I am slow and——"

"You are better here, sir," Dave answered, donning a helmet and pocketing another. "What do I do, by the way, if I want to send thoughts to you? They won't pass through this helmet."

"Take it off when you wish to transmit," the older man replied. "I will leave the instrument on, so that I will see you the instant you communicate. Good luck, Dave"—he shook his hand tightly. "If you get into difficulties, I'll try and find a way to save you."

"I know it," Dave replied quietly. "I'll succeed though, sir— never fear. And before I've finished—or rather before *we* have finished—the Intelligence is going to have a hot time of it. . . . Good-bye."

*　　*　　*　　*　　*

Nan had been upon the point of entering the breakfast room when, with staggering abruptness, she felt as though the entire floor was heaving violently beneath her feet. She clutched desperately at the wardrobe, amazed and frightened. Never in her life before had she felt so horribly dizzy; the whole room was apparently spinning round like a top. She took a lurching step forward, then stopped dumbfounded—transfixed. The room—the familiar surroundings had gone! She was in an impalpable grey mist which swirled and eddied mysteriously, horribly silent, and maddeningly opaque.

"Dave!" she shouted desperately, making a faltering step through the dense, odourless fog. "Dave! Help!"

Not a sound—not an echo. A silence allied to the infinite; a solidity that rendered sight useless. Everywhere this grey and impalpable pall. . . . Gradually Nan began to realize that she herself was normal—steady, and not in the least dizzy. She was in the grip of something as yet beyond her understanding. Calmly she stood, silently waiting. . . .

Almost at that moment it was as though she literally fell out of the mist. She found herself in a small room with black draperies, the walls lined with complicated instruments. In a moment she recognized it as the room in which she and Dave had been interviewed by Dr. Soone at the time of their entrance into the city as workers. With a startled cry she turned round on her heel, to behold the five figures before a table—one seated and the others standing.

"Dr. Soone! The Intelligence!" she jerked out, her startled eyes travelling from the cold surgeon to the massive-headed, white-faced individual seated at the table. "How did I come here? Tell me!" She strode forward towards them and spoke insistently.

"Be seated, Mrs. Elton," requested Soone smoothly, indicating a vacant chair by the table.

"I won't!" Nan replied curtly. "Say what you've got to say, and——"

"Sit down!" Soone thundered, and so imperious was his tone Nan obeyed almost involuntarily.

"You were brought here by the practical application of my fourth dimension machine," said the Intelligence impassively. "We require you for a certain purpose."

Nan's eyes flamed. "You'll get nothing from me—any of you!" she retorted defiantly. "I'm not afraid of you, anyhow."

"It is not a question of fear," responded the Intelligence in his even, unnatural tones. "You know a good deal concerning plans that have been made against me. Before you are destroyed along with your husband and that scientist Athlinstone, you are

[61]

going to reveal every detail of what they are doing, whether you like it or not. I have seen a good deal by projecting my own mind into your laboratory, but there are many things which you alone can tell me. I observe you are strong-willed. I can read nothing in your mind of interest to me—only hate for me and my companions."

"And you will learn nothing more," Nan returned coldly.

"Your courage is to be commended, Mrs. Elton," remarked Soone, with a low laugh. "The only drawback is that you evidently overlook the fact that we have machines that can read your mind. You cannot defy those. Even the Intelligence himself cannot withstand their tremendous force."

"If you refer to the instrument with which you read my mind when I first came to this city——" Nan commenced.

"I do not," Soone interjected smoothly. "I refer to an instrument three times as powerful—one which will convey every minute detail from your mind of what is going on in your laboratory at home. We chose you because your mind will be easier to read than your husband's, or that doddering chemist, Athlinstone. Guards, do your duty!"

Before she could speak Nan was seized tightly by her arms, and half carried to a tall framework, six feet in height. A succession of levers were snapped into position, and, as a consequence, steel manacles shot out of the framework and clasped her body one after the other. The remorseless clamps closed immovably about her wrists, neck, and arms, then at her waist, knees and ankles. She found it impossible to budge even a fraction of an inch without cutting her flesh.

She watched intently, trying to smother the inner fear that was slowly overcoming her, as the guards dragged forth an instrument on a tripod, fitted on rubber wheels, somewhat resembling a very complicated radio microphone. The black dial upon the front was a maze of switches and controls.

Soone motioned the guards to one side and stepped forward to the instrument, which was now directly in front of Nan. He looked at her, smiled faintly and coldly, and then switched on the power. There was no sound, nothing visible—but Nan immediately felt the awful power of the instrument. Her senses reeled as it absorbed the details of her mind and formed of it an instantaneous record. The strip of film, containing the record, was released from the side of the machine, like the tape from a tape machine, which the Intelligence studied, foot by foot.

Nan battled mightily to overcome the frightful force of the

instrument. Her head ached violently, perspiration broke out from every pore of her trembling body. . . . She made a last enormous effort . . . then sagged gently so far as her bonds would allow.

Soone cursed softly and shut off the machine.

"Fainted!" he commented savagely. "And before we got any information worth while!"

The Intelligence shrugged. "It cannot be helped, Doctor. Have her put into the next room. When she recovers we will try again. There is nothing of interest here," and he thrust the useless strip into a container at his feet.

Nan was released from the clamps and carried bodily into one of the adjoining rooms, being laid upon a couch-like affair with powerful springs. Afterwards the door was locked by electrical impulse.

Soone returned thoughtfully to the table, dismissed the guards, and then looked at the two remaining—the Intelligence himself and Eri, Secretary to the Intelligence, brilliant yet sly, crafty confidant in world-control affairs.

"Well," Soone muttered, "we're no nearer. I thought she would collapse under the strain. No flesh and blood can stand that sort of thing."

"Forget her for the time being," the Intelligence replied. "We have other matters to discuss."

"I know, but I still think we ought to conceive a way to get information from her. She'll collapse before that machine every time, and the same with the lesser one. What are we to do?"

"If the Intelligence is so brilliant as he believes, surely he can devise a means to overcome this problem?" Eri remarked, with distinct sarcasm; then he started slightly as the Intelligence slowly rose to his feet and stared at him with his deadly eyes.

"Eri—repeat that!" he commanded.

Before the Secretary could obey Soone had seized him by the shoulder, and with one fling sent him reeling against the switches on the wall. For a moment he crouched, undecided.

Soone gave a warning look and the Secretary understood. He and Soone had many things in common and more than once had the Doctor saved him from instant destruction at the Intelligence's ruthless hands.

"Don't be a fool!" Soone snapped. "You ought to know better than to make such comments before the Intelligence. Sit down here and don't speak until spoken to!"

With an unnoticed glance of gratitude Eri obeyed. The Intelligence slowly resumed his seat.

"In some things, Soone, you have a better way than I have," he commented, in his implacable voice. "We will discuss our plans for universal conquest. You know the outlines."

"I know that you have overcome the earth and seek fresh fields to conquer," Soone responded. "What is your next move to be?"

"Conquest of the Universe—conquest of the other planets that circle about us. I have derived a formula for the over-coming of gravitation—repulsory magnetic waves to be precise. Projectiles are already built. I plan to overcome the Universe, —planet by planet—that is, those which are inhabited. And after that—beyond our little system into outer space. . . ."

"I would warn you," Soone remarked, "that on other worlds you may be up against brains that will supersede your own. I will take Mars for instance. Being of older development than earth, it is possible that extremely high intelligence dwells there. That will mean intellect greater than your own!"

"I admit no intellect greater than my own!" the Intelligence answered evenly. "I have set myself out to conquer the entire Universe, and I will not be stopped. Since I have solved the secret of eternal life by discovering the antidote for the poison which creates the condition known as 'age,' I am quite immortal —will never die! If it takes me a thousand or even a million years it matters not. I shall gain my end just the same."

"You forget—we do not live beyond the allotted span," Soone commented grimly.

"You can be replaced; you are not indispensible," came the cold answer, and the Intelligence stared stonily at the change of expression on the faces of Soone and the Secretary. "Now we will discuss the plans. Eri, set the machine for recording what I have to say."

The Secretary obeyed and the Intelligence commenced, his tone monotonously irritating.

"Firstly, Mars. Reduce the inhabitants, if any, to complete subjection, and make the planet subservient to the earth. I can then spread my forces to a fresh outpost and undertake the conquest of the next planet—Venus. If any inhabitants, they will suffer the same fate—and so on, and so on. Mercury we will discount as lifeless, but the same need not apply to the outer planets, Jupiter, Saturn, Uranus, Neptune, and so forth. We may not find beings akin to ourselves, but at least we may find intelligence, which will come under my dictates. . . ."

Soone glanced at Eri as the Intelligence proceeded.

"The first projectile to Mars will be launched one month

from to-day—November 27th. The projectile will be a trial one, carrying no passengers, for I wish to see how it behaves. My instruments will record everything. If it is the success it ought to be, it is the first step in the conquest of the Universe."

"It sounds colossal to me," Soone remarked bluntly. "Not that I am in the least unwilling; I have no room for scruples and sickly sentiment. What of you, Eri?"

"It is entirely as the Intelligence wishes," came the smug answer.

The Intelligence was silent for a moment, then:

"For the present we cannot lay further plans. Bring out that girl again, Soone, and we'll see what we can get out of her. She knows too much to be safe, and every time I try and read her mind she makes her thoughts a meaningless jumble from which I cannot derive anything. Try the small machine on her."

Soone rose to his feet, removed the magnetic control from the lock of the door, and flung it open. He disappeared inside, and then returned a moment later, amazed and ruffled.

"She's gone!" he ejaculated.

"Gone!" echoed Eri.

The Intelligence rose to his feet and stalked swiftly into the adjoining room. He looked round the steel walls with his boring eyes.

"How the devil did she get out of here?" Soone asked in bewilderment. "The walls are of steel and the lock was such that even T.N.T. couldn't scratch it."

The Intelligence drew down his brows and for a while plunged every vestige of his amazing brain-power into solving the problem.

"I see them both; they are in the instrument and observing room," he said presently.

"You mean the girl and her husband?"

"I do! How they got out of here, I cannot grasp; it eludes me! Inexplicable! I cannot get to the root of the problem. Come!" He awoke to sudden action, raced swiftly from the room, and down one of the passages that led from it. Eri and Soone came close on his heels.

Presently they came into the colossal room which housed the Intelligence's amazing machines. Titanic telescopes and refractors, their tubes and lattices of steel as thick and lofty as the old-time Eiffel Tower itself, reached heavenwards; mighty whirring dynamos which controlled the instruments for harnessing the climatic conditions rose in solitary, squat, bellying masses at intervals; great bridges and stairs of steel straddled the whole wilderness of complication, to fall from the summit of which was to plunge either into the chasms of unthinkably tough metal between the engines, or drop into the heart of the merciless, whining gears themselves.

"There they are!" exclaimed Doctor Soone, pointing.

In the far distance, at the extreme end of the great room, almost hidden in a curiously bluish haze, were two helmeted figures, clambering over the colossal engines in the domed roof, through which projected the inquisitive lattice-work of the super-refractor.

"We can't stop them now," Soone exclaimed quickly. "By some uncanny means they've got out of that room and into this one. How Dave got here beats me utterly. And they're making good their escape!"

"Wait!" said the Intelligence, and staring hard at the two figures in the distance he suddenly threw every element of his enormous intellect across the intervening gap and commanded them to return. His strange eyes positively smouldered; it seemed as though little fires burned in their profound depths. . . .

The figures continued climbing. The Intelligence clenched his fists until the knuckles showed white. His jaw projected, his lips were set in a thin, perfectly straight line. The brows came down in a sharp V over the compelling orbs. . . .

Still the figures climbed upwards, becoming remote. Soone and Eri gazed at each other in dumbfounded amazement.

Perspiration began to trickle down the Intelligence's face as he strained his awful concentration to the uttermost. Then suddenly he relaxed. The distant figures still climbed on, and presently vanished from view.

"They have proven unmoved by my will," the Intelligence said, and had he been capable of emotion an intense acidity would have unquestionably flavoured his words. As it was they dropped with metallic coldness; the curious eyes flamed inwardly.

"You mean that your will was powerless against them?" Soone asked in complete astonishment.

"I do!"

"But the force you were exerting was sufficient to turn an army around and force them back to you, let alone just two human beings. I felt the power even here."

"They were not affected," the Intelligence responded. "I must retire and study this problem. In the meantime, let them go. They will not escape me in the end, even though they have done so now. Come!"

NAN slowly returned to consciousness to find herself within the dimly lighted ante-chamber of the Intelligence's own room. For a time she lay still on the well-sprung couch, then something of the confusion and dizziness passing from her mind, she gained her feet and walked silently to the door. She tested it—it failed to yield in the slightest degree. She wondered how long she had been unconscious. Suddenly she remembered the awful machine that had been trained on her mind, and shuddered.

At a sudden muffled thud against the wall she looked round with a start. Somewhere above her something clicked; then came a rushing sound akin to a loud-speaker being switched on.

"Don't be a fool! You ought to know better than pass such remarks before the Intelligence. Sit down here, and don't speak until spoken to!" This she heard.

It was the voice of Dr. Soone, clear and distinct, from somewhere above her. She wondered what it was all about. Neither she nor anybody else knew that, in his fall against the wall, Eri had accidentally pushed up the relay switch, which brought the microphone in the next room into full life and relayed throughout the whole building, to every room, the entire conversation. Had the Intelligence but been aware that every being in the vast building was listening to what he believed were his own private plans. . . .

Tensely Nan listened.

". . . conquest of the Universe; conquest of the other planets which circle about us," said the Intelligence, and gradually went through the entire conversation.

". . . and the first projectile will be launched one month from today—that is November 27th. The projectile will only be a trial one, and will carry——"

Nan stopped listening abruptly and spun round with a fast-beating heart as a something—something impalpable—began to materialize in the very air by her side.

With a slow transition the intangible became solid, and then suddenly resolved itself into the form of Dave, peering about him in the dim light.

"Dave!" Nan exclaimed in joy, and racing forward she felt herself lifted up in his arms.

"Nan—are you hurt?" he whispered, after they had embraced. "Have those swine done anything to you?"

"Only tried to wreck my mind—and failed!" she answered grimly. "But, Dave, why on earth have you got on that odd-looking helmet? And how did you get here—out of the air?"

"The fourth dimension," Dave answered. "You know that the Professor has perfected a machine to enable any of us to move in and out of the fourth dimension at will."

"Yes, yes, of course, but——"

"And that he has perfected that thought-receiving machine of his?"

"Yes."

"Well, I communicated with him by thought and explained by writing and signs that I wanted to be transported from the moors into the Intelligence's headquarters by the fourth-dimensional system. I was in too big a hurry at first to think of it. I guessed from what I had seen in the thought-machine that you were before one of those devilish machines, so I came along here by the fourth dimension. I nearly resolved into the third dimension in the next room at first, but finding you not there I altered my direction, and more by luck than judgment landed here."

"But the helmet?" Nan persisted, and as he fixed the other one over her head he explained its purpose. "Now wait a minute," he concluded, lifting his own. "I'll just give the Professor the O.K. to get us back to the lab. again."

He stood perhaps two minutes in silence, then as the pale mist gradually enveloped him and Nan again, he slipped the helmet back into position. . . . Then with an abruptness that was startling the mist suddenly vanished, and the two found themselves, not in the laboratory, but in the Intelligence's own instrument- and machine-room.

"Hell!" Dave exclaimed. "What the devil is Athlinstone playing at? We're miles away from the lab. and——"

"Never mind talk—move!" Nan exclaimed tensely. "Something must have gone wrong at the Professor's end. We've got to get out of this—and quickly."

"You're right there. Come on!"

They rapidly made their way between the roaring, ear-splitting dynamos and machines towards the immense structure of the refractor.

"To get out of here we'd better go up on the roof," Dave bawled. "After that we'll decide what to do. Come on!"

"Who first?"

"You. If you slip I can perhaps save you."

Steadily, with admirable nerve, the girl began to climb the

ladder-like steelwork, up and up. She dared not look down on the yawning gulf of deadly machinery below, dared not even contemplate the frightful death that awaited one slip, which would mean contact with those shining copper-wound cylinders, each carrying a load of tens of thousands of volts of electricity. . . .

The steel tower went up perhaps three hundred feet, on a long slant, towards the astoundingly lofty roof. . . . Suddenly Dave called a halt, and Nan forced herself to look back. For an instant her head reeled and a frightful cramped feeling came into her; then she was steady again, holding with hands that trembled a little to the cold steel.

"The Intelligence—Soone—and somebody I don't know," said Dave grimly. "I do believe the Intelligence's trying his mental stuff on us from the way he's standing." He chuckled dryly. "This is one over on him at last, anyhow. Carry on, old girl—let him wear his massive brains out on these conductive helmets of ours. Ready!"

The arduous, perilous climb continued. Once Nan slipped, and her face went white. For a time she had to pause and collect her shattered nerve; then again she struggled on. Far below, a stupendous distance, it seemed, the gleaming copper on the cylinders was still in evidence. At this height the vast roar of sound had merged into a common, bass humming, that throbbed queerly in the ears.

"Thank God!" Nan breathed out at last, clambering over the edge of the semi-circular gap in the roof. Yet even on that domed roof the refractor still projected a further three hundred feet into the air, its far distant end gleaming brightly in the morning sunlight.

On either side stretched New London, throbbing with all its usual power. The bullet-shaped aeroplanes came and went in the air-lanes with stupendous speed; here and there a helicopter rose vertically and soared away at a slightly slower pace.

"That's our best way," breathed Dave. "And we'll have to travel, too, before we're nabbed. I just can't think what can have happened to the Professor's end of the business."

The way he indicated lay across the very roofs of the city, and finally down the skeleton work of one of the aerial masts which served to control the radio-impulses which guided the aeroplanes to their landing bases. . . .

Without passing a further exchange of words the two rapidly jumped their way from roof to roof until only the control tower remained to be conquered. Here was a more difficult task. It necessitated a straight jump of four feet, or a fall to the moor three hundred feet below. They managed the task at the expense of bruised and bleeding fingers and shattered nerves. To descend the ladder in the control tower's centre seemed relatively trivial after the climb up the refractor-telescope. The only fear was that they might be observed by the control tower engineers, but all went well, and finally, pained and exhausted, they gained the solid earth, outside New London's boundaries. Here they paused for a brief respite.

"Dave," Nan said presently, laying a hand on his arm, "I've heard, authentically, that the Intelligence is going to start war on other planets, now that he has overcome this one."

"Just about what he would do. Is Soone in on this as well?"

"Most certainly. You don't expect that ambitious, cold-blooded creature to be anything else, do you? The test flights are to be made on November 27th—that is a month hence. We've got to do something about it, Dave! We can't let that monster start invading other worlds, which are probably peaceful."

"No—we can't." Dave's brow wrinkled in a frown for a moment; then he shrugged his shoulders. "Well, we can't think out a problem like that in a few minutes, and here above all places. Let's carry on and tell the Professor about it."

They stepped forward again, but at the identical moment they did so, the familiar yellow fogs of the fourth dimension silently enfolded them. When at length they cleared they were in the laboratory again, Athlinstone solicitously watching them. As they became clear to his vision he threw up his hands in welcome and incontinently embraced them.

"Splendid! Splendid!" he panted. "Dave, my boy, you did it!" He shook the young man's hand warmly. "I congratulate you! I am sorry for what happened," he went on seriously. "The machine jammed, and of course I was in a frenzy of despair lest you be recaptured. However, I worked like a mad-man and got it right again, and here you are! The danger is over."

"For the time being—yes," Dave assented, pushing a chair forward for Nan, and seating himself. "We're not out of the wood by a long way yet, Professor. The Intelligence is planning more dirty work, and if we have any respect for our planet we've got to stop him, before he finds himself up against minds which are too clever for him and brings down a rightly hostile world on our own innocent heads."

"What do you mean, Dave?"

[70]

Quietly Dave repeated what Nan had told him, and she herself embellished the details. When it was finished the old scientist sat in deep and thoughtful silence for quite five minutes.

"I thought that would be the next move," he said at last. "We will have to strain every nerve and fibre to complete that brain machine of mine. . . ."

"The trouble is that he can project his mind into this lab. and see what is going on," Nan commented worriedly.

"No, Nan," the Professor answered, with a slight smile. "You see," he explained, looking at their questioning faces both in turn, "I have found the right system by which to insulate this laboratory against thought-waves—just like the helmets on a big scale. At the present moment this laboratory is shielded by that same negative force which insulates the helmets. The most powerful mind in the universe cannot penetrate it. We are as safe as it is possible to be—and free to strain all our energies into the final great battle, which will mean either the destruction of this monster, or the end of ourselves! We have to stake—our all!" he concluded solemnly.

"I am ready," returned Dave grimly.

"Then I am too," said Nan with equal grimness. "The Intelligence must be destroyed."

"You are both young—you both have courage, as youth should have," Athlinstone murmured. "But if my brains can do it, and if the good God will help me through, I will see that there is no necessity for you two to expose yourselves to danger, with your lives hardly begun and your married life never once free of danger since the outset. It is a sin to expose youth to danger, and I shall work to a point where it will not be necessary. Now let us get to work. You, Nan, will carry on as usual—we cannot manage without your skilled hands on the domestic side. You, Dave, must help me in the laboratory. . . ." The Professor paused and smiled apologetically. "Forgive me ordering you about like this in your own home, but——"

"Rubbish!" Nan interposed, with a laugh. "Why, Professor, we look on you by now as a sort of father. Indeed, more thoughtful than many a father knows how to be," she added reflectively, and went away into the kitchen regions.

Athlinstone stood quietly looking after her for a moment, then he shrugged his shoulders and smiled. Turning, he took Dave by the arm and said:

"You've got a good and courageous wife, my boy," he confided. "See that you behave yourself!" and they both laughed.

In the next half-hour Athlinstone became the man of genius once again, moving here and there with surprising agility, controlling machines and instruments with delicate fingers, snapping out rapid, unmeaningly curt orders, assembling metal frameworks, doing a multitude of tasks with the ease and speed of a man twenty years his junior.

Between them, closely following the sheafs of plans, they slowly began to construct the metal machines in which all their hopes were to be sunk—the machine to overcome the deadly intellectual monster which held the world in its ruthless grip.

They worked on and on unceasingly, taking no cognizance of time. The point at issue was the safety of a planet, and it was a point that was ever more dominant before them. . . .

*　　　*　　　*　　　*　　　*

Three weeks later found the brain-machine completed. It had been three weeks of desperate energy and endeavour, in which the Intelligence himself had been almost forgotten. Shielded by the thought-repelling screen which the old scientist had placed over the laboratory, activity could proceed unhampered by the thought that the Intelligence knew every move as they made it. A curious exultancy filled the minds of the three at the thought of how they had so far managed to beat the intellectual colossus at his own game. Now only one week remained before the self-appointed ruler of the world should send off his first test projectile before wreaking his pitiless genius and power on unprepared and perhaps defenceless worlds.

"The preliminary tests are perfect," the Professor remarked, beaming, on the day following the completion of the brain-machine. "I have experimented to the full, and find that a steady increase in power can positively hypnotize an entire army—sufficient power can hypnotize a world to do one man's bidding. *What* a weapon! The Intelligence will never be able to defy a machine like that! Even he cannot stand against a steady and unvarying electric current."

Dave and Nan gazed at the massive boxes and switches which comprised the instrument, and then to the beaming face of the inventor hovering over them.

"You've done wonders, Professor," Dave breathed. "You're going to be the saviour of the world. I can feel it in my bones."

Athlinstone lit his pipe contentedly. "I hope so, Dave—I hope so. If not, I shudder to think of what may happen! Oh, and by the way, you had both better see how to shift the thought-repelling screen from this laboratory. We don't know what may be needed in the near future. I'll show you, too, how to operate this fourth-dimension machine of mine, so you can move yourselves in the dimension if necessary. Come along."

He moved across to the instrument-littered bench, and laid his hand on the repelling screen machine.

"This knob here is pulled out—so," he explained, suiting the action to the word. "That disconnects the current—I should say it breaks it—so that the electrical power to combat the thought-waves no longer emanates into the screen of radiation about this laboratory. This lab. is now unshielded by the throw-back screen. That clear? Good! Now, to move into the fourth dimension this machine here is used. This lever is pulled thus, and brings the angle of the fourth dimension into our own plane. The fourth dimension is a movable dimension, you understand. You step back, so——" and instantly Athlinstone vanished from view.

Nan and Dave stood waiting interestedly for his return, when a sudden slight sound behind them caused them to start. They both turned with a simultaneous movement, smothering exclamations. For against the far wall stood the Intelligence himself. . . .

"Thank you for removing the repulsive screen," said the cold voice. "I have been waiting for that for weeks. You are now both coming with me, *via* the sixth dimension, to New London. I have plans for you two! I see you are both alone," he added, looking about him.

Dave and Nan said nothing. They were expecting Athlinstone to appear at any moment, but for some reason he did not do so. Possibly, as the fourth dimension did not prevent him hearing the conversation, he deemed it wisest to remain hidden.

"If you imagine you can order us about as to what we shall do, you are making a big mistake!" Dave snapped, and jumping over to the bench he seized the two repulsion helmets.

"Wait!" commanded the Intelligence's steely voice. "I order you—wait!"

Dave struggled mightily to throw off the hypnotic power of the creature, but without avail. With a curse at his own helplessness he swung round to meet the creature's eyes, glowing and wide.

"Now—we go!" the Intelligence said; and instantly the transportation to New London was accomplished.

Dave and Nan found themselves in the council chamber of the Intelligence, with Soone and Eri already there.

Quietly the Intelligence moved to his accustomed chair and sat down.

[73]

"Now, my friend," he said steadily, "I have reached a decision concerning you both. For a long time, ever since the beginning of my rule of this world in fact, you have done all in your power to thwart me. You ought to have acquired sense enough to realize that you cannot overcome that which is your superior. You know I am superior to both of you—superior to everybody on the earth—yet you both have still persisted. There is a chance that you may stumble on something that will prove really useful to you and dangerous to me, therefore I have no alternative other than to be rid of you both. You understand?"

"I fail to see how we could help understanding," Dave replied coldly. "You're a clever man, Intelligence, and I am the first to admit it—but I still assert that the minds that made you can still find the way to destroy you!"

"One of those minds is dead, the other is my assistant, and the third one is to be exterminated," returned the Intelligence. "In face of that, what have you to say?"

"That even the cleverest make mistakes!" Dave snapped. "You may think you know everything, but there's a good deal you don't know!"

"I suppose that you think that I do not know that for the past weeks Athlinstone has been engaged on a machine capable of destroying me?" the Intelligence inquired. "I suppose, also, you think I do not know that he hid himself in the fourth dimension when I arrived in your laboratory a little while ago? Fool! I have read all that from your mind, whilst you have been standing there. I will attend to Athlinstone, and the laboratory—later!"

Dave clenched his fists but remained silent. Inwardly he cursed the day when he had conceived the idea of this monster, who was destroying the morale of an entire planet.

"To-night," the Intelligence continued, in the same impartial tone, "I am releasing a test projectile into space—as your wife already knows—that also from her mind. I have decided that there is no reason why the projectile should not carry passengers; therefore I have ordained that you two shall be placed inside that projectile—and fired into space! You will have provisions for three months, and artificial air. If the projectile lands on the planet I intend it to do, you will stand a chance for your lives; if it fails, you will die in the void. Either way you cannot return to earth, and what happens to you is no concern of mine. That is my decision."

Dave and Nan made a futile attempt to disguise their horror. They looked at each other with blanched faces. Dr. Soone smiled coldly and Eri nodded complacently. The expression of the Intelligence did not alter in the least. He pressed a button upon his desk and two guards appeared, armed with paralyzers.

"Take these two and place them in Cell 16 in the Outer Wing," the Intelligence ordered. "Mount a triplicate guard and use the paralyzers at the slightest sign of disturbance. Inform——"

He stopped suddenly and looked round as a uniformed man burst into the room without the preliminary customary knock. The fellow's hair was disordered and his eyes wildly staring.

"Sir, sir! Professor Sanders must see you at once. He——"

"And why precisely dare you burst into this room without being announced?" the Intelligence demanded.

"I'm sorry, sir. Forgive me. I was excited. Sanders has found that the whole earth is in danger!"

"Indeed? What has he discovered? Why cannot he come to me?"

"He has found that the sun is collapsing, sir. It means that the earth will freeze."

Dr. Soone compressed his lips and looked at the Intelligence.

"If this is true, it's serious!" he said grimly. "It sounds too fantastical, though. Sanders has made a mistake."

"I doubt it," Eri remarked. "Sanders is a genius of astronomy. I think, sir, we had better do as he asks."

"Very well." The Intelligence rose to his feet and turned again to the guards. "Follow my instructions with regard to these two. Now go!"

Vaguely wondering what all the conversation was about, Dave and Nan were led passively away. Dave was sufficient of a scientist to know that, if the man Sanders was correct, the earth was indeed threatened with destruction. He wished he could be present in the astronomical observatory, but such a thing was impossible. Only captivity and eventual doom, it seemed, lay ahead. . . .

CHAPTER IX   *The Fate of Athlinstone*

PROFESSOR SANDERS was surrounded by sheets of foolscap and ponderous books when the Intelligence, Soone, and Eri arrived. Instantly he jumped to his feet and looked at the three men as though uncertain how to put his thoughts into words. . . . Then suddenly he found his tongue.

"A celestial disaster is liable to overtake the earth," he said solemnly. "For about six months I have been watching certain peculiarities in the sun's behaviour and I have found that some agency, which must remain unknown I suppose, is causing the sun to collapse. . . ."

"But the theory is ridiculous," Soone protested. "Such an occurrence, if it ever happens, will be millions of years hence yet."

"Ordinarily, yes," Sanders agreed. "I have said, though that some agency is at work, possibly from another planet. This agency has the power of tearing off the electrons within the sun. . . . I see you do not follow clearly. Each star is composed of atoms. That is so, isn't it?"

"Certainly."

"Well, in the normal course of events these atoms, moving at the terrific velocity they do, will lose the outer electrons. When the last electron has gone the broken atoms will not be able to support the tremendous weight, and the sun will collapse. It will not disappear, but it will be of no use to the earth for warmth—or to any planet in the Solar System. This process would normally have taken millions of years, but somewhere in space some diabolical agency is speeding the process up, and I predict the collapse of the sun in—three years!"

"Good God!" Soone muttered.

"Get other scientists to check up on me," Sanders said. "I'd be glad of it—but see, here are the proofs. We are threatened with destruction—a freezing world—in three years. And no normal agency has brought about that solar condition! Minds, greater than ours, are deliberately preparing this disaster. It cannot be in our own Solar System, because that would mean their own planet would be doomed. It is something malignant—something beyond our understanding!" Sanders' jaw set squarely, and he pointed to the multitude of photographs and reports he had collected.

"Three years," mused the Intelligence, and gave himself up to thought. For a long time he stood rigid, exerting all his mental forces, but finally he shook his head. "There is no formula I can derive to turn away the menace," he said. "The only thing to do is to make preparations for withstanding the disaster."

"All the preparations in the world will be of no avail," was Sanders' blunt answer. "It means death—by freezing!"

"You mean there is no way out?" Soone asked helplessly.

"None whatever. Even granting we could survive for some time, our warmth will escape inexorably into the vacuum, and in time we shall perish. We have three years to live—everybody on the earth has three years to live—and that is all. Who is it that has brought about this disaster we do not know."

"And my mind fails to discover," the Intelligence muttered. "Strange! Very strange! Since there is no way out—since all preparations are useless, there is only one course. To-night I send my test projectile into space. In the coming three years we must transport every human being from this planet to some other solar system, where there is another sun. That is all."

"A colossal task, and hardly commendable," Sanders said, shaking his head. "We know of no planet beyond the Solar System which is habitable. Do you propose to go careering about in the void to find another world with the earth's characteristics on which to place our people? To find such a planet would take years—let alone the time in transporting the human race."

"Very well, then, we will leave the human race to fend for itself," the Intelligence replied coldly. "We will tell them nothing."

The other three men stared in amazement.

"But we can't do that!" Soone ejaculated.

"Why not? You forget, Soone, that I know the secret of synthetic men—the same system by which you created me. I shall take the necessary machines for creating men like myself —a few picked men—and leave these humans to do the best they can. Why should I care? They are not like myself; I have no feelings for them, nor they for me."

Even Soone was astounded. Sanders simply stared blankly, and Eri looked dazedly from one to the other. To understand the viewpoint of the emotionless, sexless Intelligence was quite impossible. This cold-blooded inhuman decision to leave the human race to death, unwarned, was almost too much for the unscrupulous surgeon to tolerate.

"I read in your mind that you will inform the peoples of the world what is happening, and give them a chance for their lives," the Intelligence remarked. "I say that you will do no such thing! If you do, I shall know, before you can perform the act. So beware! Sanders, make further observations upon the sun and send the results direct to me. I will have your conclusions verified. Come, Soone, we have plans to make now. At once!"

For once in his life completely tongue-tied, Soone followed the monster and Eri, from the observatory. . . .

The cool dusk of the autumn evening had settled over New

London when at length an armed guard came and released Dave and Nan from their stuffy little prison. He said no word and ignored all questions. With a cold and impartial dignity he conducted them from the prison building, through specially guarded ways, and ultimately to an immense quadrangle, flooded with the glare of super-electric arcs.

In the full radiance of the light reposed a cigar-shaped object, glittering magnificently. The tapering nose was pointed upwards towards the eastern horizon, at nearly sixty degrees. The dim evidence of a rope ladder was just discernible leading up to that needle-like snout. . . .

Quietly three men came out of the gloom. Neither Dave nor Nan needed to wait to discover who they were. The even tones of the Intelligence came forth, and the experts who were to watch and chart the progress of the test projectile into space, leaned a little closer. The whole affair was oddly weird. . . .

"My friends," said the Intelligence, "the hour has come when I am about to put into effect the plan I have had in mind for many years—to exterminate you both! I need not dwell again upon your chances of survival. You understand them well enough. In this space-projectile are provisions for three months —air for six. You will have no means of guiding this vessel— it will be fired into space, far enough beyond the earth's gravitation to prevent it falling back. After that, automatic repulsion waves will control it. It is aimed at Mars, and the chances of you failing to strike that planet are almost at zero. You have a chance—but on a strange and unknown world. In the vessel you will find arms to protect yourselves. I do not desire to willingly kill you; I merely wish to be assured that you can never return. Also in the vessel you will find controls that will enable you to make a safe landing on Mars—a brake control, so if you are sensible you have no need to crash to dust. My thoughts will follow you through the gulf of space—I shall be able to visualize whether or not you have made a safe landing. If you do, the projectile is a success. If you do not . . ." and the Intelligence ceased to speak with infinite significance.

Dave clenched his fists and squared his jaw. The mask-like face of the Intelligence almost goaded him to a desire for violence. Nan clung tightly to his arm. He felt that she was trembling.

"No doubt you are wondering why Athlinstone has not seen your fate in the thought vibrating machine?" the Intelligence asked after a pause. "The reason is easily explained. I have intercepted all vibrations with a machine of my own. He knows

[78]

nothing—and before long, I fancy, he will know even less."

"You mean you are going to kill him?" Dave demanded thickly.

"That hardly concerns you," the Intelligence answered coldly. "You and your wife will have quite enough on your hands to preserve your own lives without worrying over that dabbling old chemist. The poor fool ought to have known better than to try to overcome me. Now get into that projectile!"

"I won't!" Dave shouted desperately, dazed by the fact that there was no way out of the situation. He had been clinging to the hope that Athlinstone would discover some eleventh-hour method of effecting a rescue. Now, however, the Intelligence had destroyed even that possibility.

"Get in!" ordered the Intelligence's smooth, inplacable tones.

"Dave!" Nan panted. "We can't! We can't! Once we're out in space we're done for! Oh, why doesn't the Professor help us——"

Before she could conclude rough hands had seized her and borne her up to the rope ladder. Dave, fighting fiercely but futilely, came immediately after her. Step by step they were both forced up the swinging rungs, until the guards had flung them, bruised and panting, into the tiny chamber of the vessel. The hermetically-sealing clamps slid into position and the enormously thick man-hole cover became immovable and impenetrable. It could only be opened from the inside by the automatic controls, timed to operate when the projectile struck Mars—if it ever did.

"Release the machine!" ordered the Intelligence to his waiting technicians.

Somewhere a button flicked. The current shot from an unseen control board and released the power in the vast cannon-like pit beneath the projectile. With a titanic roar and colossal blast of super-heated air the metallic vessel shot upwards into the darkening sky, cleaving in a thin white line of transient heat across the faintly glowing stars in the eastern sky—and vanished.

Solitary, mysterious, never completely understood, Mars glowed in that eastern abyss. Serene in his red majesty—but grim and deadly when he became the goal for a single, unmanned projectile!

The passing days of anxiety, intense apprehension, and acute mental strain, wrought a decided change on Professor Athlinstone. Unable to leave the laboratory, unable to receive any

[79]

news of Nan or Dave by the thought-vibrator, he worked day and night to perfect some fresh device by which he could overcome the interference which was making the reception of thought vibration impossible for his machine. . . .

Instead of gaining the idea he sought, however, the strain was too much for his mentality altogether. He found he could not keep his mind on his work. He was weary and heavy-eyed, drooping through worry and loss of sleep.

Time and time again he cursed himself for a fool for ever allowing the Intelligence the remotest chance of penetrating the laboratory.

Five nights after the disappearance of Dave and Nan the old man, disheartened and bemused, was awakened from an exhausted sleep by a too familiar, metallic voice.

"Professor Athlinstone!"

He opened his eyes and blinked, rubbed them, and then sat up with a jerk upon the settee on which he had been lying. Like the phantasms of an unpleasant dream the figures of the Intelligence, of Dr. Soone, and of Eri were before him, with six silent, wax-faced guards close by.

"The Intelligence!" said Athlinstone at last, comprehending.

"Yes—the Intelligence," agreed the monster. "It has now become imperative, Athlinstone, to intercept your activities, before they become really dangerous to me. You were clever to conceive the idea of repelling thoughts; cleverer still to invent the brain-machine and thought-vibrating machine—but you have overlooked the fact that I am cleverer than you can ever be! In my hands you are akin to a new-born child!"

Slowly the Professor gained his feet and stared at the placid Intelligence with black-rimmed, sunken eyes.

"What do you mean?" he asked in a low voice.

"I mean—just this. Your former colleagues, Mr. and Mrs. Elton, are now on a journey to the planet Mars, in an uncontrollable projectile! They have a good chance for their lives, but you will never again see them on this earth—nor will any of us. You are cleverer than they are; here you have many dangerous machines. It cannot go on, Professor!"

"I will not stop!" Athlinstone retorted, thumping the bench by his side.

"If you are removed, you may *have* to!" the Intelligence countered icily. "Come here!"

Instead of obeying, Athlinstone threw himself to the nearby brain-machine and switched on the power. With a savage movement he flung the power lever into the highest notch, simultaneously throwing every vestige of his concentration into the amplifying mechanism.

"If you can stand against this, you devil, do so!" he shouted exultantly. "Come on!"

In the space of less than two minutes every member of the party began to collapse. Dr. Soone made a mighty struggle to combat the awful flow of power from the machine, but failing, he sank down unconscious upon the floor. Eri and the guards followed suit rapidly.

Only the Intelligence remained standing, his feet a little apart, his hands open at his sides. The queer eyes burned like fire once more, and down came the eyebrows into the sharp V. He took a step forward, jerkily and clumsily, as though with colossal effort. . . . Struggling mightily to hold his concentration on the mechanism, Athlinstone gave the machine all the power of which it was capable. Fear sought to seize him and upset his thoughts—fear! the element he had overlooked! He battled against it; trembled with the strain.

The Intelligence stood quite still for another long interval, his eyes staring directly into Athlinstone's. His face was wet with perspiration. The splendid forehead was furrowed with gigantic effort.

Another step . . . and another!

Fear! Athlinstone moaned inwardly. If only he had not been so weakened with worry; if only he had taken that one little, yet behemoth element into his calculations. Fear! It was to be his ruin—his end! Abruptly he relaxed with a sobbing curse. In an instant the Intelligence was upon him, and had switched off the power.

"Fool!" the monster breathed, as he bore the old scientist to the floor. "Now do you realize how hopeless it all is?"

He pulled something from his waist-belt and pointed it at the terror-stricken scientist. A faint, vaporous blue curled upwards to the ceiling, and with it went the grand soul of Rupert Athlinstone. . . .

Slowly the Intelligence rose to his feet, looked down at the gently curled, lifeless man, and then replaced his deadly instrument in his waist-belt. Going over to Soone, Eri, and the guards, he shook them into sensibility. Within five minutes they were all on their feet, gazing at the dead Professor.

"We have nothing more to fear from him," said the inhuman voice. "We will leave at once and give the order for the immediate destruction of this place and all it contains. . . . It is as well that Athlinstone, in his overwrought condition, forgot to place the repulsive screen over the laboratory," he added, looking back. "Otherwise, it might have been quite a time!"

Quietly the party left the laboratory by way of the door. Half-way across the moor two men were waiting with electrical blasting equipment.

"Proceed," the Intelligence ordered, and watched the spot where the laboratory was situated. In went the electric master-switch. A blue spark leaped the gaping enigma of machinery.

A mile and a half away a thick cloud of dust and debris shot skywards, to settle down into a thick haze which drifted slowly away on the southerly morning breeze.

The Intelligence nodded, turned about, and walked rhythmic-ally back towards New London with his colleagues. . . .

CHAPTER X   *Kal of U-Kotar*

FOR what must actually have been weeks, Dave and Nan were in a condition closely assimilated to heavy stupor, within the close confines of the test projectile. The stupendous rush out-wards from their native planet, the infinite silence of inter-stellar space, the pressure against their bodies occasioned by the ever-mounting acceleration of the vessel through the void —all these things had tended to dull their normal faculties.

Occasionally they ate sparingly, or crawled to the window to look out in the unthinkable blackness of space, upon which the stars were strewn promiscuously like diamonds on jet black velvet. For a while at least the incomputable immensities of emptiness held their minds. Each time they looked, it seemed, earth was smaller and smaller behind them, a globe of green and yellow—whilst Mars, glowing red in the firmament, swelled and expanded from pin-head proportions to a ball of sullen hues. . . .

Close upon three weeks after the departure from earth the projectile commenced to approach within close proximity to the planet. Dave, with a stupendous effort, threw off something of his terrible lethargy and held his mind down to the task of dis-covering how the brake-controls operated. It took him a full three hours to determine every detail, but by that time he was satisfied that he had mastered every intricacy.

Six hours later the projectile dropped safely to the surface of the planet, and at the impact the mysterious locks with which the Intelligence had equipped the vessel became free. Dave threw in the anchor-brake and went in to his wife.

"Well, old girl, we've landed," he announced cryptically. "We might as well be hung for sheep as for lambs, so let's arm ourselves and explore outside. I have little doubt that the air is breathable—we've pretty well proved that fact on earth. A bit attenuated, maybe, but still fit for our lungs. Just look through the window! Not an inspiring sight, eh?"

"No . . ." Nan muttered, gazing out upon a seemingly endless waste of red sand. Nowhere a tree, nowhere a sign of a habitation. Not a bird or animal. Just sand, and sand. . . . And above a steel blue sky, a flake of amazingly high cloud, and the reddish, copper sun.

Sand . . . Sand . . .

Nan shook her head. "Deathly—silent—still," she said in a low voice. "Dave, it's to be—our graveyard!"

Quietly Dave took her arm. "Don't meet trouble half-way, Nan," he counselled quietly. "Come on—let's get going."

He handed her a loaded rifle from the wall, took one himself and then pushed back the clamps of the door. As it swung open an air possessing a curious dry dustiness swept into the chamber. For a moment its thinness stung the lungs, but lost its unpleasantness after five minutes or so of deep breathing.

"Ready?" Dave asked.

"And waiting."

He jumped down through the man-hole to the sand, forgetting for the moment the lesser gravity with which he had to cope. Instead of a dignified jump to the ground he spread out sideways and fell gently on his face amidst the grains. He was only just in time to wriggle aside before Nan made precisely the same mistake.

After a time they managed to gain their feet, and practice rapidly revealed to them the easiest way of moving against the lesser attraction.

"There's one thing this low gravity does," Dave commented, as they hopped along. "It gives us about three times as much strength, as we ever had on earth, if it becomes necessary to tackle any hostile beings."

Nan replied: "I'd sooner have the gravity to which I'm accustomed and leave my strength alone," she answered. "I can hardly walk without falling. It feels like—like having little balloons tucked in my clothing. I rise nearly six inches at every step."

Silence fell between them again as they progressed. They knew not where they were going, or why. Everywhere was the

[83]

same—just the endless sand. Presently, however, there crept into the air a peculiar something—a sense of vast presences, yet invisible. The two stopped.

"You've noticed it, then?" Dave asked.

The girl nodded. "Yes—there's something near us; I can feel it. Something astoundingly powerful. . . . The air is dripping with—how shall I express it?—personality."

"You're right." Dave wrinkled his brow, pondering the queer effect; then at a slight sound he wheeled round, and Nan did likewise. What they beheld came as so violent a shock that they felt bereft of all speech and movement. They could do nothing but stare, fixedly and amazedly.

Perhaps five feet away a man was standing, apparently quite human in form, attired in robes of flowing white. A long white beard streamed down and mingled pleasantly with his snowy raiment. Masses of white hair streamed from either side of the wonderful head. An amazingly intelligent face, possessed of an expression of infinite compassion and wisdom, formed a perfect oval under the snow-white hair. It was a face that had impressed upon it countless years of knowledge and intelligence, balanced by a patience and purity beyond earthly understanding.

"Good Heaven!" Dave managed to get out at last. "Am I dreaming? Nan, it's a desert mirage—that's what it is. We're just both overwrought."

"What you see is real," said the apparition, in a voice of astounding depth and richness. It was a voice that had no terrestrial parallel, so extraordinary and bell-like were its notes.

Dave took a step forward, clutching Nan's hand.

"Who—who are you?" he demanded.

The stranger smiled faintly in response. Dave stood looking at him, thinking what a splendid man he was—upright and tall, with tremendous breadth of chest beneath his glorious beard.

"I am Kal, of U-Kotar," came the bass reply. "You, my friend, are, of course, David Elton of the planet Keznar—or, as you term it, earth. . . ."

"But you speak English; you are a being like myself!" Dave expostulated. "I had expected—— Well, anything but this!"

Kal smiled again, indulgently. "Naturally you are startled; very puzzled—but rest assured that everything will be made clear to you before long. You need explain nothing—I know it all. Nothing, my friends, can be beyond the reach of thought."

"Beyond the reach of — of thought?" Dave repeated mechanically.

"Exactly," Kal responded. "Nothing can be beyond the

power of thought. For instance, were I to command one of your earthly rose-bushes to bloom in this arid wilderness—amidst this seeming endlessness of sand, you would think me a charlatan, eh?"

Dave did not reply to that, and the old man's eyes twinkled. "Yet—look!" he said simply.

Dave turned, and an ejaculation was forced unbidden from his lips. A long gasp escaped Nan. Within two feet of them a rose-bush was swaying gently in the soft wind—a stout, healthy bush, weighted with the magnificent flowers that depended from it. The thing was a miracle—a contradiction of all known laws. The ground was dry sand, bare and lifeless as rock a few moments before . . . yet now! Dave spun round on Kal, who was smiling in his whimsical way.

"How did you do that, sir? Are you hypnotizing us?"

"Hypnotism is mental destruction," Kal responded sedately. "That bush is a manifestation of thought, which knows no barriers. Pick the rose, my son—and you too, daughter. Unlike your earthly roses, those will never die. Nothing on this world . . . dies."

Incredulous Dave and Nan stepped across to the bush and each plucked a rose. Another odd thing was the absence of thorns. A glorious perfume swept up to them as they fixed the roses in the flaps of their shirt pockets. No earthly rose on a summer evening could emit so sweet an odour as these magical creations of the Martian wilderness.

"So," Kal remarked pleasantly; then turning to the bush he just looked at it—nothing more. Yet instantly it vanished from sight and there was no trace of it in the place where it had been. Only two perfect blooms in two pocket flaps remained to testify to the miracle.

Dave and Nan commenced to wonder if they had died and this was the after life. A glance at their clothes and the distant, useless projectile destroyed the theory, however. No, Kal of U-Kotar was real enough. . . .

"Now, my friends, you will require food and drink, I observe. We of U-Kotar ceased indulging in the material practice of eating and drinking four hundred and seventy cycles ago. You, however, have not yet ascended to that level. Prepare yourselves, then, for the transportation to the City of U-Kotar, First Ruling City on the planet Eznar, City of Materialized Thought. . . . Prepare."

His voice seemed to fade away, and at the same moment the plain of sand faded also. Followed a deep purple glow,

[85]

amorphous and undetailed—then gradually a city merged into view, a city of peculiarly transparent qualities, glittering oddly in the light of the sun. Dave looked about him and found Nan by his side. They were standing upon a ledge of rock high up on the edge of a mighty natural basin. Near-by, Kal was standing, as majestic and unmoved as ever.

"That is the City of Materialized Thought, City of U-Kotar," he announced in his deep voice. "To you it looks like a city of transparence. Actually, it is not there at all! In U-Kotar, we *know* it is there, so to see it in material substance is quite unnecessary. However, now that you have viewed it from a distance, I will transport you to your chambers. Prepare."

In the space of what seemed a few seconds, Dave and Nan found themselves in an immense, delightfully cool room, windowless, but fitted with shutters on the Venetian-blind principle. To their amazement, everything in the way of furniture was perfectly earth-like. The room was almost a replica of a hotel dining-room, magnified. Tables, chairs, divans, carpets. . . . Kal chuckled slightly at the dazed expressions on his charges' faces.

"I have created this room to suit your earthly requirements," he explained. "If any detail is missing, I will proceed to have it put in order. Now, here are food and drink, also earthly."

Upon one of the tables appeared a perfectly-laid meal. A cold chicken, faultlessly cooked, lay upon a silver dish; a cold ham was there, likewise. The plates and cutlery glimmered brightly in the shaft of sunlight streaming through the window. Dave stepped forward, feeling very much akin to one who views the manifestations of a genie, and looked the meal over carefully. Nothing was missing. Even the condiments were there in silver containers.

"Sir, I do wish you would tell me how you do this sort of thing!" he exclaimed, with entreaty. "To my wife and me it is akin to magic—the sort of thing that happens in our earthly fairy stories. How do you do it?"

"Everything that appears as a miracle to you, my friends, is purely the material manifestation of my thoughts," Kal answered sedately. "Long ago we learned that it is not necessary to do so much material labour in order to bring our thoughts into the practical thing. For instance, at home, you would cook that meal and then lay it on the table. You would know at the commencement that your ultimate task would be to lay the table and put out the meal—but in the interval you would go through so much material labour in order to put that

[86]

trend of thought into practicality. Here, however, we cut out all material incidentals, and the result is instantaneous manifestation of thought. Everything is done because we *know* nothing else can obtain. As you progress in knowledge here, my children, you will follow better. For the time being, if there is anything you should desire, do not look for a bell; just think of my name, and I will come. Sleep after the meal if you desire it. You will find your rooms beyond this one—through that door. For the time being, then—farewell."

Kal seemed to melt into the air itself and was gone.

"Well!" Dave gasped at last, laughing with relief. "What do you make of this lot, Nan? We thought the Intelligence was a wizard, but, compared to this old patriarch Kal, he's an infant-in-arms. . . ."

"Yes, I was just thinking that," Nan murmured thoughtfully. "And, Dave, do you know I have an odd feeling—call it feminine intuition if you will—that the Intelligence has brought about not *our* destruction by firing us to Mars—but his own! To a man like Kal—if man he be!—nothing is impossible. He could bring the strife and trouble on earth to an end in a second. Yes, we must put the proposition to him."

"Undoubtedly," Dave agreed, then he fell into thought for a moment. "You know, Nan, it's queer that he should be a human being, in form I mean, like you and me. According to mathematical computation, the chance of beings akin to us evolving on another world is almost ten million to one against it. Insect-like beings, worm-like creatures, even plant beings or intelligent gases, are all possible—but beings like ourselves unthinkably remote! Yet here we find a human being . . . unless," he said in a change of tone, "unless he appears as a human being to make himself fully comprehensible to us. Obviously he understands everything there is to understand—our language, our planet, all about us—everything. It all seems like a dream. . . ."

He paused, ruminated, and then laughed.

"Well, we'll leave it to take care of itself," he said, with sudden abandon. "Come on and let's eat. After that our brains may be clear enough to sort out the tangle a little more easily."

CHAPTER XI   *The Plans of Kal*

WITH the passing days Kal appeared many times, always the same paradigm of beneficence, creating fresh wonders that startled the earthlings more and more each time, doing everything without moving from one spot, able to continue a conversation whilst issuing a dozen thought orders simultaneously. Undoubtedly Kal was the consumate example of mind's unquestionable control over matter, a control as earthlings have hoped during generations to achieve.

Then came the day for the audience with Kal before the ruling council of the city. Dave and Nan were transported in the usual mysterious fashion, and found themselves finally in a vast hallway, surrounded by tier upon tier of learned, grave-faced men, all of whom possessed wonderful beards. Like serried rows of Druids they rose upwards to the magnificent roof—yet there was noticeably absent that air of criticism and searching eyes inseparable from a similar earthly gathering. Dave and Nan felt the atmosphere to be one of peace and content; it was like a draught of pure, cold water to a thirsty man.

Kal himself quietly advanced to a massive seat in the exact centre of the room.

"Now, my friends," he said in his deep, even voice, "the time has come, when we are to understand each other to the full. Or perhaps I should say, when you are to understand *us* to the full. There is nothing about you or your planet we do not know. However, to come to the point. You remarked quite recently to your wife that repetition of beings like yourselves on any other world is a very remote chance. Quite correct. We beings, in reality, have no form at all. We are merely thoughts, invisible to lesser intelligence, but fully understandable to ourselves. For your edification, however, we have all agreed to assume human form like yourselves so that you may see and understand us. We all knew of your coming here long before you arrived, nor need you fear any hostility on this planet, my friends."

Kal paused for a moment, and then resumed:

"On your planet there is considerable strife and unrest owing to the activities of a being you created—the Intelligence, is there not?" he asked.

"Yes," Dave muttered. "When I got the idea for making an intelligent being I never thought I was sealing the doom of humanity. That monster plans to stop the growth of the human race and plans the making of a synthetic race of beings like himself."

"So I am aware," Kal nodded. "He will not, however, succeed in his efforts."

Dave took a step forward. "Sir, do you mean that?" he demanded tensely. "How do you know? I know you possess unlimited powers with your complete mastery over matter, but——"

"You have had proof of the attainments of the people of U-Kotar," Kal responded, with dignity. "I have said that he— or it—the Intelligence, will not succeed. We of this planet are out to prevent it. We have seen many things you would not understand, and have devised many things you would not understand. Your earth is a sister planet to ours—she needs help, and needs it badly. We are an older race, millions of years older, and so millions of years older in knowledge. We alone can help, and are going to. It was we who put the idea into the mind of the Intelligence to send you two to Mars, as you call it. We thought it would be as well that you understand what is to happen. You have heard, perhaps, on the earth, that the sun is threatened with collapse?"

Dave nodded.

"We are causing that," said Kal calmly. "We have marshalled together irresistible cosmic forces and are deliberately wrecking the power of the sun—a task which it will take three of your years to accomplish. It could be done instantaneously, but we prefer it otherwise. We have decided that your planet must be purged and swept of every manifestation of the Intelligence and his adherents. You must learn to begin all over again!"

"But in the collapse of the sun all the planets will suffer— this one included," Dave commented.

Kal smiled faintly. "There are some things you do not understand, my son," he said indulgently. "The other planets have been provided for by us. What life dwells on them is of such order as to be amply arranged for. No—your earth will be frozen out, will become a dimly lighted, ice-bound planet, incapable of holding life—for a time. In that time every element of evil, every trace and ramification of the Intelligence, will be wiped out of existence . . . Then will come a change—the sun will recover; and those same cosmic forces that destroyed the sun will bring another sun into being. Question not these forces; they are so mighty that even we cannot understand them to the full. Suffice it that nobody on the earth will suffer save those who deserve to. Our plans are such that the Intelligence will be powerless—how this will come about we alone know."

Kal paused and considered for a moment.

"It will be your duty, my children, to do as you are commanded by me. You are to trust solely to my judgment."

"Willingly," Dave said, and Nan nodded assent.

"Very well. I shall put you both back on the earth not by rockets or projectiles—but by the power of thought. During this transportation two and a half years shall pass by. There is no time in thought. You can be in the future as well as in the present, if you but understand it. Therefore, while you are in a state between worlds, so to speak, I will put my plans into operation. You will find yourselves on your own world again, but two and a half years will have passed by. All that you have to do is to entirely follow what seem the dictates of your judgment. Actually, it will be my judgment at work. No matter how dangerous your position may seem, do not fear, for I shall be with you. At the approach of the time for the solar eclipse you will find that the earth is honeycombed with underground refuges, and into these will be herded all the deserving peoples of the world. I will see that you have but little trouble doing this. I will be by your side, invisibly. After the cold, you will see the good that has been done, and will see a new earth, upon which you must all start anew, the better for experience. You understand?"

"Perfectly," Dave nodded. "It is needless for me to add that I don't see how you're going to do all this."

"That is not your task," Kal returned. "If you are ready, my colleagues and I will commence your transportation back to the earth. . . ."

"So soon!" Dave exclaimed.

"Why not?" Kal asked quietly.

"Oh—no reason at all. It just seemed sudden."

"You are limiting yourself to time, my son—a grave error. There is no such thing as time, therefore we bid you—farewell. And do not fear, for I shall be with you."

Dave and Nan caught a last glimpse of his wonderful old face and inscrutable eyes, then the deep violet enigma to which they were now accustomed closed in upon them, and they seemed to be buoyed upwards into an immense and limitless abyss. . . .

CHAPTER XII   *The Last of the Intelligence*

"So you say there is no further information from Mars?" Dr. Soone enquired of the Intelligence.

The monster aroused himself from a deep concentration and looked at the surgeon. An expression, the closest to anxiety

Soone had ever seen on that emotionless visage, was upon the Intelligence's face.

"No," he answered tonelessly. "For a reason which my mind cannot fathom all communication between me and the man Elton and his wife has been cut off. I saw them land safely on Mars; I saw them walking across a desert of red sand—but now, just a blank! I cannot learn anything about them or the planet. I confess I am puzzled."

"But surely nothing is a puzzle to such a mind as yours?" Soone explained. "Perhaps—perhaps they are dead?"

"That would not hinder me viewing the planet," the Intelligence responded. "No, there is some force at work deliberately interfering with my attempts to connect with the planet.

"It may be—a mind greater than my own!" and the face set into hard lines.

Soone did not answer that question, for it had been put in such a tone as to preclude interrogation. Instead he said: "Since communication is impossible, and you know those two arrived on the planet, and cannot therefore get back, why bother at all? We have enough trouble of our own to contend with.

"Sanders gave me a report today on the solar business. It is quite true. The sun will collapse in three years' time.

"What are you going to do about it?"

"I have already answered that question, Soone. We—that is, myself, you, Eri, and a group of experts on synthetic men—will wait until the disaster is about to happen. Then we will make for the void which lies beyond our own solar system, find a suitable planet, and finally commence to create a race akin to myself—intellectual giants."

"And leave the human race to destruction?" Soone asked.

"There is no other way. The lesser must ever fall before the greater. To tell them of our plans would endanger our chances—to tell them of the solar disaster, that is to come, would make an immediate demand for shelters of some kind. No, the best way is a secret departure, when it is too late for them to realize the danger. I have had reports circulated to the effect that any rumours of solar disturbance are to be ignored as pure gossip."

Soone shrugged. "Well, you know best," he said indifferently. "After all, I'm not particularly concerned in what happens to them."

"I have given instructions to the projectile works to have a very large projectile complete with all controls made as soon as

[91]

possible," the Intelligence continued. "So soon as that is done I shall have the ship put in a secure place, where it cannot be tampered with—in readiness for instant departure. And, so soon as that ship is built, I personally shall destroy the plans so that no other machine can be built and pursue us."

"Who is in charge of the plans?" Soone enquired.

"Eri. They could not be in safer hands," the Intelligence replied.

"I agree with you there. I just thought how fatal it would be for us if the news or plans got to other ears."

"No news will leak out," the Intelligence responded. "The plans I lay are always perfect . . ."

And so the days passed on—days which lengthened into months, and months into years. The steady, organized precision of New London went on apace. Hints and vague suggestions of impending solar disaster had reached the workers, despite the belief of the Intelligence that every avenue of information had been effectively closed up. The workers paid but little heed, however. One or two thought about it, but did not act. Everybody was content, believing that the information was false. The Intelligence himself was at his post, and he surely would be the first to remark if anything untoward were threatened. . . .

The workers only began to wonder if there was anything behind it all, when terrific electrical storms began to sweep the earth from end to end, the overture to the eventual collapse of the seriously unstable sun. Yet what danger could there be? Again came the thought—the Intelligence himself was at his post.

On the night of March 16th, 2044, the Intelligence called Soone, Eri, and six picked men into his chambers.

"My friends," he said, "six weeks will see the collapse of the sun. Already indeed the first titanic storms preceding the actual collapse are ravaging the earth. It is no longer safe to stay. I will not waste time on words. Come with me, to where the private underground workshop is situated."

"Why?" asked Eri.

"To enter the projectile of course," the Intelligence responded. "What else did you think?"

Eri smiled slyly. "A good plan, Intelligence," he commented, "but not quite good enough. What are you going to say when I tell you that I have had a dummy ship built and destroyed all the plans?"

"You . . . what?" Soone gasped incredulously.

Eri smiled again, venomously. "So you thought I'd follow out your orders to the last, eh, Intelligence? You inhuman swine! Do you think I forget the way you've treated me all through the years? Do you think I'm afraid to turn the tables on you? Not I! I've got you into a jam from which you can't get out—and, above all, it was I who spread the rumours among the people, and they want—*you!*"

"You traitor!" the Intelligence snarled. "You traitor! You know the penalty for this?"

"I don't mind," Eri returned languidly. "Kill me if you want. I shall die in any case soon, so it might as well be now. I've yearned for years to be revenged upon you, and now I've done it! So you can go to hell, and——" He ceased to speak. He crumpled up gently and silently before the death ray instrument of the Intelligence.

"Now to the workshop!" the Intelligence commanded in a voice of steel. "If Eri spoke the truth, we are trapped. There is a chance it was bluff. Come!"

They filed out hastily, but at the door of the underground workshop they were met by two men armed with paralysers.

"What is this?" the Intelligence demanded. "I gave no permission for you to stand here. Out of the way!"

"Just a moment!" commanded the foremost man. "Take a good look at me, Intelligence—you too, Dr. Soone. Who am I?"

Soone stared and then jumped back as though he had been struck. "My God, David Elton!" he gasped out huskily.

"A bit of a surprise, eh?" Dave asked pleasantly. "Just try and think out how I have come back from Mars. This 'man' here is Nan, my wife. It may interest you to know that Eri made a dummy vessel, not by the dictates of his own mind, but by the dictates of the master-mind which transported my wife and me across space back to this planet. Intelligence, you have met your master in a being known as Kal of U-Kotar, and——"

He stopped short as the Intelligence whipped out his death ray. The button shot into position and Dave waited stoically for the end he was not to find. For some strange reason nothing happened. With a face of iron the Intelligence examined the control and then flung the instrument to the floor.

"Jammed!" he said in an icy voice. "Men, seize these two and have them put in prison . . ."

The men hesitated; the paralyzers were levelled at them.

"So the paralyzers scare you?" the Intelligence asked them. "I will do it myself, then," and he threw himself into a spell of

[93]

enormous concentration. As time passed, however, and his mental powers seemed completely without effect, he came as near to impatience as his unemotional body could do.

"Get out of my way! Time is precious!"

"I've no objections," Dave answered, "but you know your space machine is useless. And the workers are looking for you, too! You're cornered, and you may as well realize it! So what are you going to do?"

Before Dave could grasp what was happening, the Intelligence and Dr. Soone had both turned on their heels and were fleeing down the passage-way as fast as their legs could carry them.

"Why the devil don't you put us in the fourth dimension?" Soone panted desperately, as he tore alongside his superior.

"I cannot! I cannot!" the Intelligence muttered. "Something has happened somewhere. My mental powers seem useless. Make for the machine-room . . . we'll turn a brain machine on this rabble."

Behind them, Dave, Nan, and the guards followed like the wind, up passages, clambering up stairways, through rooms, down aisles, between machines, and at last into the great machine-room, the nerve centre of New London.

Panting hard, the Intelligence jumped to his brain machine, Soone by his side. He flung over the power lever breathlessly.

Not a sound. The machine refused to operate . . .

"For God's sake!" Soone panted hoarsely. "Turn it on! The whole lot of them will be on us in a minute!"

"The mechanism's jammed!" the Intelligence returned savagely. "My machinery seems to be all out of order. Good God, Soone, I do believe I'm sinking down to the level of an ordinary human being. I have human emotions coming over me—fear, hate—I have lost my former enormous mental range. I can think no higher than you can. Listen! I've become an ordinary man!"

"It's a fact!" Soone breathed in awe, looking dazedly at the now wild and furious Intelligence. "You're like us—you are a human being—no longer synthetic. . . . They're coming! Quick! Up to the roof out of the way."

At full speed they rushed along the aisle and commenced the ascent of the refractor telescope.

At that moment a babbling roar commenced to fill the edifice. Voices shouted in furious anger, resonant thumps, and the thunder of running feet. At the same moment a sea of dark blue figures surged into the immense machine-room, bawling at the top of their voices.

"The workers!" the Intelligence panted. "Get on, Soone—quick—or we're done!"

Soone turned to continue, then to his astonishment an iron grip seized his shoulder. He was amazed to find that the Intelligence was gripping him, a wild light suddenly flaming in his strange eyes.

"Listen, Soone!" rasped that metallic voice; "you were the man who made my brain, who moulded me—and it is you also who are responsible for my inevitable destruction! Somewhere you made an error; you made my brain capable of collapse under extreme strain. Every movement I become less intelligen—I am sinking through the scale of de-evolution, back to the primitive . . . am descending to the beast. But, by Heaven, if I am sinking, you shall go too!"

"Have you gone mad?" the surgeon panted, fighting to free himself.

It seemed possible that the Intelligence had indeed relapsed into insanity. The mighty mind was no longer the slave; it was the master. The Intelligence was no more; he was naught but a fighting, screaming savage, blind to all sense of reason; a struggling maniac amidst the ruins of a shattered mind . . .

Soone fought mightily against the ruthless arms that held him. He punched, and wrestled, and kicked. All to no avail. The Intelligence was as mighty in ape-like strength as he had been in mind. Soone screamed hoarsely as he slipped over the edge of the girder upon which he was standing and hung for a moment in mid-air.

"Pull me up! Pull me up!" he shouted desperately.

The Intelligence returned the plea with a snarling grunt.

Soone sank lower and lower, then quite suddenly the Intelligence overbalanced and he and Soone toppled through the air—a sheer hundred-foot drop.

On the ground floor Dave and Nan, surrounded by the fascinated workers, saw the two forms hurtle downwards straight on to the gleaming copper-wound cylinders of the electrical generators. . . . At that moment of impact there came a dazzling blue flash and a sharp hissing noise. An immense short circuit passed throughout the entire mass of machinery, and it whined to a standstill.

It seemed like a silence promoted in gratitude to the passing of a giant intelligence and its creator.

Upon one of the giant cylinders lay two piles of grey dust, which stirred in the gentle breeze through the open doors. . . .

WITH the passing of the weeks, and the iron control of the Intelligence at last removed, the workers looked pitifully for guidance in their hour of need, and Dave came into his own. Aided by a quartet of highly intellectual men, late enforced minions of the Intelligence, he succeeded in getting the entire army of workers into a semblance of order, put them into divisions, and knew, by the end of a month, exactly where each division was situated.

It was at the time he had succeeded in arranging all these divisions, that the earth was suddenly found to be a mass of underground shelters, carefully stocked with food, water, and artificial air—enough to last for months. Kal had kept his word. What the workers thought of this miracle was never discovered, for the approach of the solar collapse was too imminent to permit investigation.

The people obeyed orders without question, and within a week every man, woman, and child had vanished from the face of the earth, were living, deep underground, in perfect comfort, yet able to view the outside world through snub-nosed towers of unbreakable glass. ·

Dave and Nan, accompanied by the intellectuals, had a special underground residence to themselves, completely equipped with instruments.

Three days before the actual collapse the first evidences of something amiss became apparent on the earth. Thunderstorms of incredible violence swept the planet from end to end.

Being within clear view of New London, from that high point once known as Parliament Hill, Dave and Nan watched in awe the gradual collapse of that mighty city. Tower after tower vanished in vast crumblings of masonry and steel as the blue-white bolts stabbed down from the inky clouds. Rain descended in torrents, pouring off the glass tower of the residence in rivulets, forming into pools in the dusty soil. . . . Then, just as suddenly as they came, the storms would diminish and allow the sun to shine forth—an angry, red-looking sun, inflamed and sinister. . . .

On the third day, at 2.14 p.m., according to Dave's chronometer, the disaster came. At that moment the last electron was wrested from the outer shell, and the disrupted atoms could no longer hold the weight of the sun. What happened could not be seen owing to the dense clouds that had gathered, but everybody became aware of an encroaching dullness that deepened into twilight, until the afternoon was as cheerless and gloomy as one hour before dawn.

The exterior thermometers registered two degrees drop in twenty minutes. Dave and Nan, with the intellectuals, sat watching the proceedings, calculating and checking notes. Whatever the cosmic forces were that Kal had brought to bear, they had certainly achieved their object. Somewhere behind all the clouds a weakly glimmering sun must be shining—but bereft of all its normal warmth.

Then came storms—terrifying, fearful storms. Angry and deadly uprisings of Nature that flogged the earth unmercifully. The vast alteration in the sun's behaviour brought about such colossal upheavals as would have been deemed impossible. Whirlwinds and tidal waves swept and flooded the earth with a fury that knew no bounds. The sea, lashed to a savagery, which had no parallel in earth's history, crashed inwards on the land, wiping out villages, flooding and ruining cities, sweeping away entire cliffs, and roaring as a colossal ruinous monster of destruction over the wind and rain-lashed landscape.

The Thames, from the viewpoint of Dave and Nan, changed from a flooded ribbon of dull grey to a sudden mighty lake at the uprush of the sea from its mouth. Triumphant the waves rolled on, carving New London in two as though with a vast knife. The rain, also, formed itself into rolling rivers and tumbled down in frothing cascades to meet the swirling sea in the valley below.

Chaos, supreme and irresistible.

Then with the passage of the hours, the fury of the electrical disturbances abated somewhat—and finally ceased altogether. The earth became enshrouded with a deathly calmness for a space.

Outside lay an inconceivable scene of havoc and destruction. New London was nothing but a tottering ruin, entirely awash. The sea, fortunately—or was it something more than fortune? —had confined itself to the valley below, isolating the southernmost parts of England—turning them into an island upon which no being lived or moved.

Towards evening a glimpse of the sun was obtained. It lay low down on the horizon, oddly distorted by atmospheric irregularities—a ghost of a sun, pale and wan, with not a trace of heat. Its light was more powerful than that of the moon, but its heat-giving qualities were entirely absent . . .

It set at last, sinking, as it seemed, into the now subsiding sea.

With the coming of darkness the thermometer commenced the downward fall in earnest. It dropped to the freezing point an hour after sunset, and down to zero three hours afterwards. A wind sprang up about this time, a wind that brought with it a blizzard of unprecedented force. Peering through the gaps in the glass, which had escaped frost spangles, Dave could see naught but a white and glassy waste outside, and a writhing, seething chaos of white flakes. He hardly needed to guess that the clouds had condensed with the cold. . . .

What took place after the coming of the great blizzard nobody could say. Day after day passed without any visible sign of daylight. It seemed as though the sun had gone altogether. The mercury of the thermometer had dropped so low that it had disappeared entirely from the tube. Outside there was only the moaning of the ice-charged wind, and a dim, roaring sound, that spoke of a perpetual destruction going on in the deserted, ice-bound world beyond. . . .

Days passed into weeks, and still there was no sign of daylight. The people underground waited and waited, patiently—all view of the outside world blotted out. They lived comfortably, contentedly, unaware where it was all going to end, content to live their lives in the brilliantly lighted underworld with their friends and families . . . .

To Dave, however, leader of them all, the situation began to present grave fears.

"I can't understand it!" he muttered. "The earth is frozen from end to end by this time—there can't be a spark of life left in it; and we know that during the disasters in this darkness vast transformations must have taken place . . . But why doesn't Kal keep his word, I wonder!"

"He will keep his word," Nan murmured. "Don't worry, Dave—it'll all come right. And—— Look! What's that!"

She clutched his arm and pointed through the one tiny clear gap in the glass. Dave stared and began to breathe hard.

Far away to the east lay a band of pale grey, caressing the horizon. It widened slowly and changed colour by imperceptible degrees . . . Grey—then muddy cream—then pure white . . . and at last, blue.

"Blue!" Dave shouted huskily. "Blue sky! Look!"

Gradually the blueness spread outwards and upwards, expanded into an ever widening gulf, until the blackness overhead seemed like a mountain range in silhouette against it.

The earth beneath shone silvery white as the blueness spread. Everywhere lay ice and snow—a fairyland of glittering, coruscating pendants . . . Came a beam of light at last; yellow light, powerful and warm.

Dave shot a glance upwards.

"A sun!" he threw out excitedly. "Not our sun, but a smaller one—just as hot and powerful, though! We've won, boys! Kal has kept his word . . ."

Yet withal, it was many days before the temperature rose far enough to permit of outside exploration. So soon as it was safe to venture Dave gave the order for temporary evacuation in order to examine the situation.

And what a situation it was!

Not a stick or stone was left standing. Everywhere was just a chaos of collapsed edifices and shattered, unrecognizable landscape. The snow, rapidly melting, had caused world-wide floods, and altered the entire topography of the globe. No land was as before. No land had a building standing. In one mighty effort Nature had obliterated everything man had cherished and possessed. New London was but a memory, far under the new coast line—all manifestations of the Intelligence, his wonderful cities, his marvellous creative forces, had been wiped out of all comprehension or knowledge. . . .

Dave shook his head slowly as he looked down at the sea where New London had been.

"Well, perhaps it is as well," he murmured. "We've cleaned up everything, and the world can—start again."

Thanks to the organized system to which the amalgamated races of the world worked, the task of building up new cities and charting new countries was not so gargantuan as had at first been expected.

Even so, five long years passed before the signs of really appreciable order arrived—years in which Dave and Nan toiled almost unceasingly to help and instruct the people, and years in which the collapse of the old-time sun was forgotten and done with.

Within ten years the world was practically back in a normal position—at least far enough forward for Dave and Nan—acclaimed, without question, Joint Presidents of World Reform—to take their well-earned holiday, whilst trusted advisers continued their activities. . . .

For their holiday they chose the countryside, green and fresh with the glory of early summer, the rays of the new-born sun slanting down, hot and life-giving, between the trees.

"Well, Nan, we've had a packed life," Dave murmured, idly throwing a stone into the river at his feet. "And to think it

[99]

could all have been stopped if I'd listened to you!"

"We learn by experience, Dave," Nan murmured; then she gave a laugh. "But think of the wonderful things we have seen —and done! These roses, for instance. Over ten years old, and they smell as fresh and sweet as the day when Kal made them appear. I shall carry mine to my dying day."

"And I too, dear girl," Dave smiled, looking up at her.

"It is well," commented a profound voice.

The two looked around, up the bank, startled—then they gasped with amazement as they beheld none other than Kal himself coming slowly down the bank towards them, attired in his customary costume of white and gold, and seeming not a day older.

"Kal!" Dave ejaculated at last. "By Jove, sir, but I'm glad to see you again. Your words proved correct."

"Naturally," the old Martian returned pleasantly. "I have merely come to bid you a last farewell. You have done well, my children—you have seen for yourself that only experience can teach a necessary lesson. Don't interfere with Nature again, son—that is my advice; the advice of a mind millions of years ahead of you. Watch that, and you have nothing to fear. May you have contentment now until the end of your days . . . Farewell—for ever."

"But——" Dave began; then he stopped as the vision of Kal faded slowly from sight. He looked back at Nan, perplexedly.

She smiled at his expression. "Why worry, Dave? You do not pretend to understand Kal's powers, do you? He is right—experience is the only teacher."

"Yes." Dave threw another stone and looked back at the girl, the sun shimmering in her fair hair, "Yes! Man is God-given, God-made, and God-sustained. . . ."

The girl's grey eyes looked back at him, then she sank her chin on her hand and looked pensively away across the river.

"Yes, Dave, you're right. Nature is self-sufficient. I have you, and you have me . . . so all's well with the world!"

And as if in confirmation, a bird took up a thread of silver song in the tree above her. . . .

THE END